"Vern Smith's 'The Gimmick' is about a hard-nosed cop, a bombshell in a belly shirt, and a bank machine card scam. It's a complex and intense story, and who can resist the brilliant opening?" – Philip Alexander, *Front & Centre Magazine*

"Smith's tale of not-so-small-time crooks with a knack for draining other people's bank accounts and the bumbling cops on their tails (one of whom is among the crooks' victims) is a flat-out riot. Punchy dialogue moves the story. Humorous human characters bring it life. The plot is solid. Smith sets the bar high."
– Matthew Firth, *The Ottawa (X)Press*

"Wilderness meets the city in 'The Great Salmon Hunt,' Vern Smith's delightful, wicked tall tale. Men fish for monster-size salmon on Lake Ontario while in the distance, 'The city core, the SkyDome, the CN Tower, and the Gardiner Expressway were enveloped in a green plume of smog, as if a lime rainbow had wrapped itself around downtown.' In *Concrete Forest*, the city is wilderness." – Zsuzsi Gartner, *Quill & Quire*

"Reading Vern Smith is to be reminded that urban America is more than the sum of its con jobs; it is a texture built of rips and stitches, a circus tent under which some of its wackiest animators hold forth—from Phyllis Diller to Carl Stalling, from Erich Sokol to Ishmael Reed. *The Green Ghetto* is electric, eccentric, extracellular madness."
– Michael Turner, author of *Hard Core Logo*

"*The Green Ghetto* is a model for modern westerns. Witty and socially conscious, it's a needed update for a genre that long ago rode off into a dire sunset." – Nick Pearce, *Broken Pencil*

"It's enough to make you think the story of the rise and fall of urban Detroit and the rise and fall of the American prairie farm were linked in some way, that the same mythos is at work in the cycle of both. In other words, Vern Smith does what great writers do. He takes his own narrative, masterfully woven and orchestrated, and makes it matter beyond its own story . . . (*The Green Ghetto*) is a highly recommended new read."
– Adam Van Winkle, *Cowboy Jamboree*

"A humorously unadulterated look at life in post-9/11, war-on-drugs America and Canada."
– Ben Vassar, *The Michigan Daily*

"A beautiful mix of genre and literary fiction. The dialogue and prose snaps, crackles and flows down the page at a breakneck pace. Smith has put together a wild, comedic romp with literary overtones." – Tony Nesca, author of *Junkyard Lucy*

"Vern Smith is running right up front with the heavy hitters of American fiction."
– Roland S. Jefferson, author of *The School on 103rd Street*

"Classic noir mixed with fresh absurdity."
– Theodore Carter, author of *Stealing The Scream*

"Pynchon meets Elmore Leonard and they nip on over to Canada."
– John L. Sheppard, author of *Small Town Punk*

"A keen cultural eye." – Nicholas Rys, *Toledo City Paper*

"Needle point descriptions and subtle plots give this book (*Glue for Breakfast . . . and other stories*) an aire of truth and reality . . . Smith has written a brilliant work, and I can't remember reading something that has drawn me in as this did. I kept thinking about William S. Burroughs, but Vern Smith has a voice of his own."
– Dave Palmer, *Upstate Magazine*

"Toxic alienation runs the reader into the sensuous oblivion of inner-city life. Vern finds beauty in ugliness and glamor in losing . . . Growing up in the shadow of Detroit obviously had a profound effect." – Ziggy Lorenc, City TV

THE GIMMICK

NOVELETTES, STORIES, AND SKETCHES

BY

VERN SMITH

Cover by Gretchen Jankowski

ISBN: 978-1-7333526-0-4
Run Amok Books, 2020
First Edition

RunAmok

Printed in the USA

Acknowledgement of previous publication and production

"Texas Egg" originally appeared in *Qwerty*. It was subsequently published as a chapbook in a signed and numbered edition of 100 for a Wench Films fundraiser.

"The Day Carter Killed Harvey in Bellevue Square" originally appeared in *Black Cat 115*.

"The Gimmick" originally appeared in the anthology *Hard Boiled Love* (Insomniac Press) and was shortlisted as a finalist for the Arthur Ellis Award.

"A Safe Existence on the Outskirts of Town" originally appeared in *Zygote*. It was subsequently published as a chapbook by Black Bile Press in a signed and numbered edition of 100.

"Theater in an Empty Room: a one-act play" originally appeared in *Queen Street Quarterly* and *Burning Ambitions: the anthology of short-shorts* (Rush Hour Revisions). It was subsequently produced as a multi-media installation for Toronto Arts Week by Wench Films.

"You Need Something to Slow You Down" originally appeared in *Schrödinger's Cat*. It was subsequently published as a chapbook by Belly of the Beast in a signed and numbered edition of 100.

"Letters of Support" is being adapted into a cinematic short by Troublelight Films.

"The Great Salmon Hunt" originally appeared in *Glue for Breakfast...and other stories* (Rush Hour Revisions). It was subsequently published in the anthology *Concrete Forest: The New Fiction of Urban Canada* (McClelland & Stewart).

"An International Incident" originally appeared in *BULL*.

"Natalia Cauzillo's Last Ride Out" originally appeared in *Zygote*. It was subsequently published in the anthology *Corporate Catharsis* (Paper Angel Press).

TABLE OF CONTENTS

For Debbie, who walked the walk

The extended dance mix of "Killing Me Softly" plays loudly from an overhead speaker, too loudly for a Monday morning. It's fall, early November, steady rain outside. I'm sitting two tables from LeClerc, waiting for my dirty dishes to be cleared. I can't see the clock from here, so I'm not sure of the time.

LeClerc has been busy reading and re-reading The Last Temptation's menu, turning it over, back, not tempted by much. Nonetheless, when Pauline stops at his table a fourth time, he is finally ready.

"The special," he announces, referring to the menu item with his index. "Only I want three eggs—not two—over easy. Charge me extra."

Pauline nods, scratching at her recently peroxided pageboy hair. "Bacon or sausage?"

LeClerc gets introspective, or at least that's the impression I get from his sigh, then a look of deep thought. "What kind of pork do you have?"

Pauline closes and opens her eyes slowly, says, "The kind that comes from pigs."

LeClerc smiles. "Alright."

"Alright, what?"

"Both."

"Both?"

"Both." Leclerc nods sagely. "Like I said, charge me extra. And real hash browns this time, not French fries."

"Okay then." Pauline makes a note of it. "What kind of toast? Brown or white?"

"Hmm." LeClerc pauses before saying something sure to further complicate the transaction. "Whole wheat."

"Brown," she tells him firmly, grimacing, scribbling.

"But no butter." LeClerc raises his hands, waving both for emphasis.

Pauline refers to her notes, the corners of her lips tugging. "You're kidding, right?"

"No." He shakes his head in jerks. "No butter. None."

She jots it down.

"And do you have any A1?"

"HP?" Pauline says questioningly.

He nods. "Good enough, and could you please ask them to play something a little lighter? A crooner, perhaps. And bring me some cranberry juice; half cranberry juice, half water. Coffee… Honey, too."

Pauline flips the page and takes the last of her notes, relieving LeClerc of his menu, then clears my table.

Seconds later, "Killing Me Softly" is abruptly removed in mid-beat, replaced by a soothing Dean Martin platter, "Tik-A-Tee, Tik-A-Tay" up first.

I haven't seen LeClerc for some time. Until today, I'd begun to assume he'd left the market under dubious circumstances. Even though I don't know him well, I make a point of thanking him for his initiative.

"Somebody had to do it," I tell him. "The la-la-la part was starting to irritate me."

"And not just a little." He waves once at my approval. "It's the repetition. Besides, Petula Clark would never have been okay with that."

I mutter something about club kids, forgetting the white zip-up boots, red vinyl mini, and Special K T-shirt Pauline is wearing. She is back just as the exchange ends, avoiding my line of sight, like she heard me, quietly delivering LeClerc's half cranberry juice/half water along with his coffee.

LeClerc doesn't drink the concoction right away. Instead, he mixes honey into his coffee, the spoon rattling in his cup. He begins sipping, staring vaguely into an off-kilter tapestry stretched out on the far wall. He can plainly see an Egyptian thing going on in that tapestry. There are elephants and horses and dozens of exotic Egyptian women striking exotic Egyptian poses, walking just like exotic Egyptian women are supposed to walk. Given that they are all identical, I figure the scene is sure to have offended someone, or that it will. That's probably why LeClerc holds his chin like something is striking a chord.

Maybe, I think, the tapestry simply tells the story of a king who fell in love with his servants—all of them. Maybe that's what LeClerc is thinking as he unwraps an orange Halls, plopping it into his mouth. Clicking it on his teeth, he rolls his tongue to get at the flavor and the mentholyptus, whatever the hell mentholyptus is, exactly. Next, he shakes the second last cigarette from its soft pack, lights up, smoking, smoking to the filter.

Appropriately, Dean Martin lyrically commiserates his own cigarette shortage while LeClerc crushes his butt in into an ashtray. At that, he withdraws the partially dissolved lozenge from his mouth, placing it neatly on top of his cigarette package, saving it for his last smoke.

Ten, maybe 15 minutes later, Pauline serves up his breakfast, as negotiated.

LeClerc, he approves, clasps his hands together, says, "Perfect."

Shaking her head, Pauline promises to return and freshen his coffee, only she calls it java. By the time she's back with the pot, LeClerc is putting the finishing touches on his meal. The eggs, hash browns, bacon, and sausage are now sliced, diced, and mixed into a makeshift casserole of sorts. Half the HP is gone; thrown into the mix, giving the meal a rusty tinge.

Brown furrowed, LeClerc concentrates like a neurosurgeon, meticulously slicing the pulped food into tinier and tinier slivers.

Pauline tops up his cup, mine, too, then she is gone.

As for Leclerc, he appears to be finished with the preliminaries. He's looking over his mash like he's about to bless it, seemingly taking careful stock and wondering if something could possibly be missing.

It was mid-afternoon, somewhere around two on a sticky Tuesday, late July. Carter's transistor had been calling for rain since breakfast, but humidity thickened the air. The sun beat down, radiation intake up, and everyone was going on like winter was a long-lost relative.

There would be no relief for weeks.

Out in Bellevue Square, Carter sat on his green bench, as he would, refusing on principle to fight the heat. He'd been cold and sick all winter, so he wasn't going to complain. Not now.

The square was the closest thing he ever had to a backyard, something of a miniature park—a parkette, they called it—with a circular wading pool in the middle.

Adjusting the brown and tan satchel slung across his chest like a newspaper bag, he sat alone on the pool's north bank, facing the sun. Across the water, about a hundred feet away, sat Fitzgerald on the southern extreme. The pond's geyser shot up in between them, keeping the water cool.

Shithawks circled like the poor man's buzzards, waiting for Fitzgerald's afternoon ritual of breaking stale bread into tiny bits, then tossing the bits onto a concrete shore near the water's edge. The pigeons would come soon, and they'd come up close, always too close.

* * *

In the beginning, there were no angles, no agendas, and no vendettas. Back then, it was just about killing seconds and minutes and hours within the neighborhood's confines. But quite some time ago, it became a merciless grind in a place where the year always seemed to be 1977.

Carter and Fitzgerald, the two of them never spoke, not once in all those summers—going about their ways in detached manners, developing a deep, mutual, brooding hate based entirely on the nonverbal.

It gave them purpose, Carter thought, and reason, the intangibles needed when they were alone, always in the heat when it was too much, shivering in their rooms in the winter, which was most of the time.

Somewhere inside, even Carter silently acknowledged Fitzgerald's feeding ritual, why it needed to be done. And why they needed to be there, together, in a space forever getting tighter.

Fitzgerald had been feeding the birds that whole time, drawing them in. With a steady sustenance supply, the shithawks and pigeons made nearby nests. It only made sense. The square was a source of people food, and Fitzgerald was among the most dependable of his species.

All of that was fine by Carter, to a point. He understood hunger, and he understood middle-age crazy. He knew what it was to be declining in the middle of the day—the fear of nothing to do and a limited supply of discretionary dollars to do it with. So yes, a man had to do something. But the filthy birds had become too much, and Carter was not alone in his distress.

In the late '80s, the city put up signs aimed at discouraging Fitzgerald and his kind from offering up their scraps. When they refused to cease and desist, city workers took a run of their own, feeding the birds drug-laced nuts and seeds. It was a touchy-feely bureaucratic compromise that satisfied no one. The feed was supposed to agitate the birds and drive them away, without killing them. But they picked the narcotic crumbs clean, looking back at the city workers, and, in their own way, asked for more.

They were always asking for more, and they kept coming back like diseased derelicts, fighting over hard bread, expired produce, rancid bits of meat, and whatever else thrown at them. Seemed like a lot of people weren't finishing their hotdogs, so Carter thought the birds were distressed by their diets, their tiny assholes bunged up. That what they were eating was responsible—all that yeast rising inside—for the tousling and fraying. Some were so badly beaten he figured that self-produced body paste held their feathers together, their poor little systems working overtime to stem the disfigurement.

Fine. They needed help, like everyone else. But whenever Fitzgerald's supplies began looking grim, they'd swoop down like vampire children on everyone else.

Carter never asked for that, any of it, and he never brought anything for the birds. He wasn't going to encourage feeders when excrement speckled the square, contaminated dabs of oil paint everywhere.

Pigeon droppings, Carter had learned, were among the most toxic animal-produced substances—he'd heard it on the transistor—not to mention displeasing from an aesthetic point of view. And he felt he'd reached and surpassed the point of being reasonable. He'd been dive-bombed too many times, including four hits that summer. Sure, it was supposed to mean good luck, but Carter couldn't see how getting shit on had improved his life at all. If anything, he thought maybe the birds were making him sicker. It had gone on for too long, and now there were too many shithawks, too many pigeons.

It wouldn't have been a federal case, certainly not the silent war it had become, except that afternoons in Bellevue Square were among Carter's last pilgrimages in a life that didn't work out quite the way he planned. He needed to be in the square. It was his refuge, his sanctuary, a place to go and get on, listening to his radio and trading stories with friends only his mind brought to life. Utterly and simply, it was a place to be.

* * *

Carter's transistor reported a bad score from the ballpark. At this, he accidentally burned himself with a cigarette. Sucking on the sore spot, he'd forgotten how much those tiny burns stung, wondering how he'd managed to avoid them for so long. In addition, he was somewhat sure he was sun-tanning a cancer burn—a dark blotch the size of a dime on his receding forehead.

Turning brown just like last July and every other one of the past 20 summers, he remembered that item about the ozone hole. News had it right over the city. At least, he thought that's what the transistor had said.

True or not, Carter knew it wasn't safe to be out in the sun. Then again, it wasn't safe to drink the water, eat the food, or even fuck, and he didn't want to exist in a place where just the living was like being on the edge of a free-fire zone. So he did all those things, when he could, enjoying at least a little control over something that couldn't end well.

Over on the pool's southern end, Fitzgerald kept tossing moldy feed. Pigeons materialized, joining the shithawks and turning the square into a rent-controlled Jack Miner's of sorts.

Back to the North, Carter felt like he was melting inside, burning some more. Glaring across the way at Fitzgerald, smiling a smug fuck-you back at him.

* * *

The birds were cooing and squawking and eating when Scagleoni showed at his regular time. Claiming his bench on the wading pool's west bank, he buried his face in his arms.

Fitzgerald thought he was laughing to show disrespect but couldn't determine who it was aimed at.

Carter thought Scagleoni was weeping because he was wearing

impractical clothing—long polyester sleeves, heavy navy pants, and insulated desert boots that would have been appropriate six months ago.

"Get the fuck outta' here," Scagleoni snapped, shoo-shooing a group of birds away with the back of his left hand. "There's nothing for you... Nothing."

From the north and south polars, Carter and Fitzgerald faced each other, twitching every so often inside walking shorts and T-shirts turned drab and from too many cycles.

Scagleoni considered himself a failure, Fitzgerald a deadbeat. Carter fancied himself an ambiguous blend of the two. All of which meant they had more in common than not, except for the fact that Scagleoni often spoke out loud. In their minds, both Carter and Fitzgerald knew that this particular flaw would lead to Scagleoni's demise. He'd do well to make it through another summer shooting his mouth off like that. And there he was, oblivious to it all, having another mood swing. Jabbering now, trying to entice the birds without the benefit of bait.

"Sing, little eater men. S-I-N-G. Peter Peter Peter..."

Scagleoni thought about his wife, wondering where she'd been for the last three days, why she had to go. Trying to stop thinking of her, his voice drifted off, fading.

North, Carter picked himself up off the bench. With a limp, he was walking and stumbling and balancing en route to the fountain. Pressing the button, he let the water flow, working it down from lukewarm to cold. After 33 seconds or so, he held the satchel to his side, lowering his mouth toward the spout. White droppings fermenting on the device like digested white lightning stopped him halfway. Ended up he mumbled something about salmonella, encephalitis, bottled water, and conspiracies, all in a single breath.

Shuffling back to his bench, he saw Fitzgerald's offerings picked clean of anything substantial. Only the smallest crumbs remained. The birds would be dispersing soon.

But before the pigeons and shithawks had an opportunity to fly free, Carter reached into his satchel, producing a transparent bulk-bag of croutons, sprinkled with something that looked like parsley. Figuring they were mass-produced to complement Caesar salads, or to be stuffed into the rectal cavities of rapidly decomposing fowl, he threw them around aimlessly.

With the first handful hitting the concrete, Fitzgerald's fair-weathered flock scattered in a stormy blur of city-snow-white-and-X-mas-green-and-Easter-purple, swooping down and squawking north. Pecking with reckless abandon as Carter doled out the pungent feed.

He smiled, glowing as if post-coital while the transistor sent out a warning to the investors of junior mines. What? Like, senior mines were okay? Once the business report was complete, failing to answer Carter's most reasonable query, a hard-driving dance tune that seemed to be called "Hobo Humpin' Slobo Babe" tested his discount speakers with a deep bass. The song slowed, a woman singing about candy on the shore, something about being left for dead, dead for good. Then the men started singing hard and fast again.

Carter did not know what a hobo humpin' slobo babe was, exactly, but it made him think about a fashion program on TV—smoke machines and amazon go-go dancers wearing thigh-high boots, black leather.

Yeah, what with Carter embracing his ways, Fitzgerald knew something was wrong. His mouth hung open, confused, eyes pinched as he processed the situation. Croutons were too expensive for this type of thing and Carter had too many, considering he, too, had to be on a fixed income of some sort.

Worried, Fitzgerald wondered if his stale bread would be good enough for the vermin next time. Ego-bruising aside, he was twisting and turning on the outside now. He knew Carter hated his birds, and, over time, the more Carter hated them, the more

Fitzgerald fed them.

That was just the way it worked, and whenever Carter became obviously animated and affected, Fitzgerald would leave the square, only to return minutes later with a new supply. But Fitzgerald's cheque would not arrive for at least another day. And he was right out of cheap day-old product when Scagleoni grimaced, chanting.

"GO BIRDS GO...GO BIRDS GO..."

On the east bench, McLaren arrived, kicking off sandals with thick rubber straps. She reached into the hip pocket of her baggy jean shorts, checking to see if something was there. Feeling it, she sat back, wiggling in a burnt-orange tank top, *enerchi* embroidered across the middle of her chest. She stopped when the left strap fell, exposing a vanilla line on her shoulder.

She was younger than the others, somewhere in her late twenties or early thirties, but Carter never could tell about these things. Whatever, he watched her join in on the shrieking, without bothering to understand the situation, drowning out Scagleoni.

"GO BIRDS GO...GO BIRDS GO..."

Fitzgerald felt the first signs of coming undone. Walking in circles, ulcer burning, he wanted his birds back. In search of spoiled food, he ran into a Thai restaurant across Augusta. Back on the sidewalk seconds later, he was ejected over yet another long-running feud. This time, the guy in the apron was calling 911 for sure. Fitzgerald was too upset to listen, tearing apart the garbage out on the curb. The guy in the apron said he was really going to do it, Fitzgerald rummaging for something, anything.

"GO BIRDS GO," Scagleoni and McLaren screamed in foggy unison.

Jackhammers tapped in repetition from the job site three blocks away. Dickie Dee jingled. And the continuous smell of decomposing flesh wafted into the square from chicken-blood alley.

In front of Fitzgerald, a flat-black Chevy Malibu turned over, backfiring, belching a cloud the color of its paint.

"GO BIRDS GO..."

Kids played on the swings and the pollywog teeter-totters. They climbed on the jungle gym and the monkey bars and slid down the yellow tongue of the lizard slide. They made makeshift castles in the sandbox, yelling the things kids yell, making that collective noise they make without actually forming words.

"GO BIRDS GO..."

Dickie Dee and his bells crept closer. Carter waded into the pool—that being what it was for, after all—washing the dust of crouton crumbs from his hands, then washing some more.

"GO BIRDS GO..."

Good and clean, Carter pushed his gimpy legs back towards shore, almost falling when he motioned Dickie Dee over.

Some old guy bummed a cigarette off some other old guy.

A young couple made out under an evergreen tree.

"GO BIRDS GO..."

Fitzgerald came running across Augusta holding a crate of rotting tomatoes he'd salvaged. Only he forgot to look both ways, trapped in the center of the street by a blaring horn when the Malibu clipped him just enough to knock him down, tomatoes rolling into the gutter.

"GO BIRDS GO..."

Fitzgerald regained some semblance of his surroundings, picking himself up, gathering a half-dozen of the soggy tomatoes. As best he could, he came running like a three-legged dog across Augusta, screaming. Just like the children, no actual words were formed.

"GO BIRDS GO..."

An elderly widow decked-out in black walked by the pool on her way out of the market, her groceries in tow on one of those contraptions with wheels.

Carter found enough change in his pocket to pay Dickie Dee, unwrapping his ice-cold treat, watching the widow pass a brown-skinned man holding a red-and-green umbrella, the flag of somewhere or another.

"GO BIRDS GO..."

It seemed like any other day in the neighborhood.

Out the in the middle of the water, Harvey was floating face-down with some of the others—all city-snow-white-and-X-mas-green-and-Easter-purple—as Fitzgerald splashed to him in hurried want, dropping the tomatoes in the water, crying and calling the bird by the name he had given it.

On shore, two dozen or so convulsed on the cement. A few more—mostly hearty shithawks—managed to fly away in wounded flight, determined to die in a place of their choosing. And Christ, those two near Carter's feet. He was satisfied they all had the fever the way they were pecking at each other.

Scagleoni started screaming about something else—he was going to take off all his clothes and run around naked if someone didn't turn down the heat—and McLaren was quick to promise the same.

On the North side, Carter sat back down on his bench, thinking McLaren should do it, sucking on a cherry popsicle in the sun, watching Harvey and the others bobbing in the water. Behind his back, the first angry clouds started rolling in just as his transistor called off the storm-watch.

1

Cecil Bolan started believing he really was tougher than a dozen years in jail. At least that's how all-news, all-the-time had been describing him since the verdict came in.

Nine months earlier, Cecil and his partner Alex Johnson arrested three men running a telemarketing office on Bloor West. Their scheme revolved around soliciting application fees for loans aimed at folks with bad credit. Up front, prospects paid $75.99 as a sign of good faith. The hook of it came when they were told their credit was too damn bad.

Always too damn bad.

Today Charlie Summerhayes, Lowell Cunningham, and Killean Jones had been found guilty of swindling more than 2,600 people out of $180,000 or so.

All-news, all-the-time probably wouldn't have made much noise about Summerhayes and Cunningham. But this Killean Jones was supposed to be into loan-sharking, racketeering, extortion—even if nothing stuck. That's why two fraud cops were throwing themselves a party at Fran's, a little diner near headquarters.

"First time ever the HNIC gets four years," said Cecil. "Going to the bad prison. Kingston."

"HNIC?" Alex put his beer down. "I hope you're talking about Hockey Night In Canada."

Cecil's smile buckled. "Head Nigger In Charge."

"I'm right here, junior."

"Wasn't talking about you."

"Just all those other niggers," Alex said. "Huh?"

Forget Alex, Cecil told himself. Forget that anti-cop city councillor accusing him of going a bit Steven Seagal during the sting.

"And Cecil, you should not have done that with the pepper spray," Alex said. "Do only what is necessary, I keep telling you. Putting Alex in a bad spot. You've got to be objective out there. See the criminal as a client, a customer."

"Yeah, yeah, yeah." Cecil waved his hand back and forth. "You heard the man on the radio. 'Tougher than a dozen years in jail.'"

Alex took a pull on his bottle. "You about as tough as a merry-go-round bronco. Smart as one, too."

"You heard all-news." Cecil smiled again, laughing like he wasn't going to let Alex spoil the sweet. "And that city councillor, I'd like to see her do my job for a day. Besides, what are they saying about you? Nothing."

"That's what I mean. I don't want my name on the radio. Had to lie my ass off. Say I saw Killean Jones go for a letter opener before you seasoned him. What if they had a camera or such shit? Cop in jail on perjury is everyone's bitch. As it is, I'm listening for footsteps."

"He's four years in jail." Cecil held up the appropriate number of digits. "They're all three of them four years in jail—Cecil's dozen. Man on the radio said that, too."

"Forget the man on the radio. You don't want to be on the radio on account of a man like Killean Jones has friends, money, options. And he's still crying entrapment."

Cecil didn't acknowledge that. He wanted another beer. But the waitress was changing shifts, time for money to exchange hands.

Fran's Interac system wasn't online with the credit union, so Cecil slipped out through an alley to Grenville Street. Could have saved time and went to the CIBC, but that would have cost a dollar. So long as he used the credit union, withdrawals were free.

The association had held out on that clause.

Smells like piss for a change, he thought. Stepping into the kiosk, riffling through his wallet, locating his debit card. He slid it into the automatic teller, looking into a mirage of blues and greens and golds, waiting for his PIN prompt. Instead, the machine deemed itself out of order, temporarily.

Just give me the card, he thought. Pay the charge somewhere else.

But the machine wasn't spitting up his digital bankroll, and that had Cecil pushing buttons, any button. Ready to punch the thing when he noticed her in the screen's reflection.

"Out of order," he said, turning to a messy blonde with tortoise shell glasses. Her lime halter was covered in daisies, exposing a pretty stomach, just a bit round. Light crow's feet around her eyes crinkled when she smiled. It was kind of nice seeing an old broad keeping her shit in a pile. No, it was encouraging.

"Machine ate my card," he said.

"Been acting funny." She adjusted hip-hugger bell-bottoms from where the waist had been cut off, eye-shadow-blue G-string riding high. "Same thing happened to me Friday. Woman at the credit union, Sara. You know Sara?"

Cecil shook his head, beer high fading. "Sara say what to do?"

"Yes. Like I said, this happened Friday. On my way to dinner, VISA's maxed—"

Cecil, turning his right hand over in a roll, said, "Yeah, yeah, yeah."

"Sara told me if that happened again I needed to key in my PIN twice, hit cancel."

Cecil followed directions. Punched in his PIN twice. Hit cancel. Nothing—nothing. "The hell Sara say now?"

"Punch in your PIN twice, cancel." Pressing her shoulders forward, up. "That's all."

Cecil was pushing all the buttons now. "My card."

"Call Sara in the morning. Tell her you were talking to Amy Alcott. Tell her Amy Alcott said they ought to spend the hundred bucks and have it fixed."

Cecil walked past her saying something about the CIBC at Yonge and College. She followed as if to go there, told him again to call Sara first thing. They went in separate directions at the alley where Cecil stopped to light a cigarette. Inhaling, looking across the street, he watched a fancy ponytail man—case worker or a welfare lawyer, something like that—in a paisley vest, Levi's, and clogs. Heading for the kiosk.

Cecil thought about yelling something, then walked back into the alley. "Fuck it." He looked around, alone. "Smart bureaucrat like that ought to figure it out."

2

"First you cry that Fran's Interac still isn't hooked up to the credit union, like it's news," Alex said. "Now the machine ate your card? Whole story has more holes than your average Sammy Davis Jr. plot."

Cecil held up three fingers. "Told you thrice."

"So tell me again, all of it."

Cecil recounted the events at the credit union. Alex taunted him, laughing—laughing until the part about the lime halter-top giving Cecil some very valuable instabanking guidance.

"You're telling me that a lady, bare stomach, stood there next to you as you punched your PIN twice? Told you to do it and you just did it? Even if this is all, hmm, a coinkidink, how much of that Nova Scotia beer you been drinking?"

"Six, seven."

Alex fingered the bill to Cecil. "Says here you had nine Keiths next to my five Millers. Your beer is also times and a half."

"Not quite."

"Close enough, Cecil, close enough. Especially now that you don't happen to have any cash money handy."

Cecil held his hands out. "Just buy my beers, Chrissakes."

"Look, if you're saying it like it happened, I think you just been played on the Windsor Withhold. Or maybe that's just what you want me to think."

"Windsor Withhold?"

"If this is the same animal, yes. The Windsor Withhold. A real, true-to-life thing. Old as you is mad, Cecil. Man in Windsor started it in the '90s. Around the casinos. You put your card in the slot, only it does not come back on account of he put a plastic envelope in the machine to withhold it from you. Was around here a few years back, couple months, then just cut the damn thing out. Smart. Professional."

"Professional?" Cecil chopped at the air. "Real, true to life thing, huh?"

"I'm telling you, call your bank."

"Credit union."

"Whatever, call and cancel your card."

Cecil pulled his wallet out of his breast pocket, removing a stack of cards. He went through the first row and started another, stopping halfway, pointing. "You're the same guy told me Jacqueline Susann was kidnapped. That her hands were cut off, sent to her agent."

Alex looked away, biting down. Covered his jaw, but Cecil could see it clenching through his fingers.

"I told that story a dozen times before I told Frieda," Cecil said. "She reads that crap. *Valley of the Dolls, The Love Machine.* Thought me knowing something obscure like that would impress her. You know what she told me?"

Alex shook his head, wrapping his arms around his shoulders, struggling in his charcoal suit. The cut was tight, correct.

"That Jacqueline Susann died of cancer."

Alex put up his hands. "No, man. I'm serious." Letting it out. "It's for real. The Windsor Withhold." Pounding his knee. "Real, true-to-life thing."

3

George Barnes and Deanna Gould had sublet a two-bedroom on Rawlings for the summer from a pair of interior design students. The so-called avenue was more of an alley; their apartment one of three in a converted coach house. Except for the windows, almost every inch of the rectangle, even the air conditioner and the exterior outlet, was covered in Virginia creeper.

The unit itself was a little tight—more like a big one-bedroom that had been sectioned off into a two—furnished with kitschy stuff from garage sales. Mostly, they needed the corrugated metal shed outside to pass for a garage. Paid an extra fifty to hide their ride.

Inside the master bedroom, Deanna had six candles going, incense. George thought it was jasmine, but then he didn't know jasmine from catnip.

"Good gimmick," he said. Sitting on a rocking chair in house shorts and a mustard bowling shirt, eating pad Thai out of a box. "But where do we get the plastic sleeves?"

"Sports collectors shop." Deanna was distracted, cueing a Joan Jett tape. "They're for baseball cards."

"Baseball cards?"

"Yeah, first the card goes into the soft sleeve like the one we use. If they're really valuable, they then put the soft sleeve containing the card into a hard sleeve. Still haven't figured out how to use one of those yet, the hard ones."

"How the fuck did you come up with it?"

"Dad collects baseball cards. It was our gimmick, really."

"That's great." He stabbed a shrimp with a chopstick. "Great fucking gimmick."

"But honey."

"Yeah?"

"We've got to come up with a new one."

"I like this gimmick. The gimmick's good."

"Cops are smarter than you think. Get in, get out. That's what dad always says, and he never got pinched once."

"Yeah okay," George said. "Brainstorming starts in the ayem. Let's just enjoy the night. What're you doing in there anyway? When do I get to see?"

"Stay there."

She hit play, wishing it could always like this. George started to say something about counterfeit cheques, cutting himself short when he heard "Crimson and Clover," their song, looking side-ways.

I, now I don't hardly know her

But I think I can love her

She was mouthing the words Joan Jett sang, standing in the hallway next to a four-foot Jade plant, arms crossed. The wig was gone, hair red again, or something. Christ, it was orange. Without pancake powder and glasses her face was splattered in freckles all the way down to her cleavage.

"Can I get away with this?" she said.

"You could pick Kojak's pocket wearing that. Let your arms go."

"Turn down the lights, George. Fuck sakes—let your arms go—I'm 44."

"Baby, no turn out the lights. You're beautiful. Don't have to be 21 to be beautiful. And Christ, I'm gonna be 36."

"Long way from 44." She dimmed the switch, turning, dropping her arms. Wearing a stewardess uniform, or rather some Frederick's number inspired by a stewardess uniform. A pastel-blue skirt rested on top of her thighs. The matching jacket had been cropped at the fourth or fifth rib. Up top, a little cap with bronze wings stood off kilter. It bounced off his knee, spinning on the hardwood as she leaned over to give him a peek, kissing him.

4

Frieda Bolan had left for work by the time her husband woke up parched. He downed a bottle of Sudbury Springs from the fridge. Took a nice, long, hard piss. Called the credit union after that. Asked for Sara.

There was a pause, lady muffling the phone. "Is there a Sara works here?" She sounded more confused when she asked again. "No Sara," she told Cecil. "This is the civil service credit union. That's where you're calling. You know that?"

Again, Cecil explained. "...Then she said to tell Sara Amy Alcott sent me. Said to say Amy Alcott said to go ahead and spend the hundred bucks and get it fixed."

"Like I said, no Sara. And Amy Alcott is a professional golfer, five major championships. Sure you got the right names?"

Cecil massaged his temples, his shoulder cradling the phone. "Can you just check if my card's in the machine? Machine ate my card."

Further investigation said Cecil's card wasn't at the credit union. He was also $2,000 short. Overdrawn.

"But isn't my limit a thousand?"

"That's right," she said. "A thousand dollars a day. A thousand dollars was withdrawn at 11:50 on July 9th. That would be last night. And again, a thousand dollars was taken at 12:02 July 10th, this morning. A thousand dollars a day."

"And I'm on the hook for all of it?"

"Afraid so, sir. Effectively, you gave out your PIN when you allowed this woman to stand at the screen with you and followed her directions. That is in your contract—that you can't communicate your PIN in any way. Should I cancel your card?"

"What do you think?" Cecil slammed the phone down.

5

This was the part that kept Alex Johnson interested—playing Jehovah, educating, looking across his desk.

"Cecil, you're a pretty boy with waves of dark hair the ordinary man'd cut off a nut for. Give you that. Wearing a real classy three-button suit with side vent and square shoulders, Italian style, that Alex picked out for you. But you still can't bring yourself to respect the professional and that makes a young man a liability, this line of work."

"Save the speech." Cecil put one hand up. "Just tell me how this Windsor Withhold thing works again."

"Windsor Withhold, yes. They take a small plastic envelope— just yay bigger than a bank card—and fit it into the card slot." Alex paused, throwing back three acetaminophen tablets, washing them down with one of those four-dollar coffees, foam and cinnamon sprinkles. "When the mark puts his card in—"

"Don't call me a mark."

"Fine, when you put your card in, machine knows it's there but can't read it. That's the beauty. Get the machine to tell itself it's out of order. That's when the lady tells you to punch in your PIN."

Cecil brought a hand over his eyes.

"So she's looking over your shoulder reading your PIN. Just to be sure, you do it again. She needs verification." Alex tapped the side of his head. "Take nothing but your intelligence. You probably watch her walk down the street. What was it you said that one had on?"

"Halter," Cecil said. "Flares with low-rise hip-huggers. No, the flares were extra low-rise. Had the waist cut off." He remembered the G-string riding high but left it at that.

"See, you didn't tell me all that. You know why she does that? Cuts off the waist, that is."

"No, but I'm sure you're going to fucking tell me."

"Same reason Mariah Carey does it."

"Singer went loco in the coco?"

"Yes, the Mariah Carey. She has boy hips. So she cuts off the waist to create the illusion that she has lady hips, a little bit anyway. Same thing here. Con wants you to see hips. Give you something to look at while you run through the drill. That's the diversion. Once you see her round the corner, all you can think about is hips. Hips, hips, hips. Or maybe a smart guy like you, you're thinking about what you're going to say to the credit union. Drafting a letter in your head about how their shit doesn't work. Meanwhile, her boyfriend—maybe the guy with a ponytail, in this case—moves in and grabs your card. They make one withdrawal before midnight and another right after."

"But the machines. They've got cameras. It shouldn't be this tough."

"That's right, most of the time anyway, and under normal circumstances we'd have prints within the hour."

"Well, why don't we?"

"Because you belong to the credit union. They took a poll and members found the technology, hmm, Orwellian."

"Orwellian?"

"Fuck Cecil, I find it creepy and I'm a cop. Read an article saying they take the average man's picture 27 times a day. More like 33 for a black man. Besides, if these are the same folks from Windsor, they know a disguise. Professional."

"Professional? For a $2,000 job."

"Make that $2,000 a pop. They ran that play 10, 20 times last night. Makes them 10, 20 times more successful than today's average bank robber. Professional. Just kept walking down Yonge Street making their play, a crime of repetition."

6

George and Deanna spread out on the tan sectional, drinking Corona, eating blue corn chips with salsa. *One Flew Over the Cuckoo's Nest* was the afternoon movie, just at the part where Jack Nicholson mounts a protest because the crazies aren't allowed to watch the World Series. Jack was imitating a baseball announcer when the station cut to a spot for antibacterial dish soap.

"That's what's creating the superbugs," Deanna said. "Just a bit of soap. That's all you need. Soap."

News update jingled next. The anchor was wearing suspenders. He was almost ready. "Police are looking for a couple in their late thirties..."

George pointed at Deanna. "Good on you."

"...in connection with as many as two dozen stolen bank cards last night in the downtown core."

"More like 18," said Deanna.

The anchor nut-shelled the gimmick, reporting almost $30,000 missing from accounts of those played last night and this morning. Deanna's blue-green eyes studied George.

"More like 25." He maintained contact with the anchor, sliding his right hand into his grey Everlast boxers. "Didn't have the right number of cards, or your age."

"Among those taken was fraud detective Cecil Bolan." The anchor smiled like someone cracked a joke into his earpiece.

"We got a cop," Deanna said. She was wearing two-piece karate-style pajamas, bunching the brownish-red material together below her neck. "A cop. That's not good."

"No, baby. That just means we're real good. That's all."

"Don't baby me. The gimmick is tired."

"The gimmick's good, baby. We're just becoming famous. The Windsor Withholders."

"Look, George. It's my gimmick—my dad's gimmick, too—and I say we have to start breaking in something else."

"We will, baby. We will."

She looked at him, cross, pointing her chin at his crotch. "You wanna leave some for me."

George looked back, what?

"Get your hand out of your pants."

"In a related matter..." Footage of a black man filled the screen, his expression neutral. He was shaven bald, as if to highlight a thinly shaped moustache and brow. Saying "No comment," leaving a salmon-colored building.

"... Killean Jones and two other men found guilty for their part in a Bloor Street telemarketing scheme were released on bail today after an Ontario appeals court decided to hear their case. Following continuing allegations of entrapment and brutality, court said..."

Deanna pointed. "That's the guy I was telling you about. The guy dad worked with."

George looked hard, squinting. "This Killean Jones looks like a pretty bad dude. You say your dad worked with him? What'd your dad do with him?"

Deanna thought about it—that stretch in '93 just after the Windsor Casino opened. Back then, the government gaming house was located in a temporary home, the old art gallery, and security was learning on the job. Busloads of tourists with rolls of cash, it had been easy for dad. "They just did some work together, regional stuff where one of them needed the other. When one of them needed a man out of town."

"Like what?"

"Jobs, scams—the usual—you know."

"No, I don't know," George said. "Specifically."

"Specifically, I can't tell you."

"Can't tell me? You're supposed to be my for-always girl, and you can't tell me?"

Goddammit, Deanna thought. "It's my dad, George. Not my place to be telling you what he did."

George cut his eyes at her, shaking his head like he was half-way into a pout. "People in love—and fuck I love you—especially people like us, you think Bonnie kept secrets from Clyde? I don't think so."

Deanna stood, leaning over him in the loose two-piece outfit. "First of all, George, don't make the mistake of turning this into a test of love. Think of it as a confidentiality agreement between me and dad. Second, Bonnie and Clyde stole millions—and that was in 1930's American money. Us, we've just lifted a few Canadian bank cards. So, until they're writing folks songs about us, let's just be George and Deanna, okay?"

"But baby, I just want to know—"

She put her hand up sharply, stopped him. "You should be happy I don't tell you. I tell you about dad, why wouldn't I tell him about you? 'Oh that George, setting me up to play a copper.' I tell him you did that to his little girl and he'd put a gun in your ass. That's the test of love—keeping a lid on stuff like that. Protecting you, protecting him, get it?"

George didn't say anything.

Seeing him sunken into the couch beneath her, she tried to

draw his attention elsewhere. Pulling the belt on her top, opening it, gently tossing her arms back, letting the garment slide. The bottoms hung loose, low on her hips, revealing a G-string riding a few inches above.

"Why do you do that?" he said, focused. "Wear the G high, pants low?"

"Curves." She looped her fingers through the sides of her G. "Old girl like me, I don't exactly have child-bearing hips. Wearing the pants low and the G high, it creates curves. Why? Don't you like it?"

She pulled the belt out of her trousers, letting them drop, gathering around her ankles. Dangling the belt across his face like a feather. Then, wrapping it around his neck, she knotted it hard and tight, taking off down the hall.

George gagged, tugging at the knot and jumping up, chasing the soles of her feet, slightly dirty from the hardwood. She was a stride or two from the bed when she turned to face him. He was diving at her, coming down on top of her.

"I thought I was being romantic," he said, holding her shoulders and leaning back. "Thinking of us like Bonnie and Clyde."

She rolled her eyes. "Clyde drank a dozen Cokes a day, had bad teeth. You think Bonnie did him like I do you?"

George figured that Bonnie must've. That it was why Clyde was robbing banks all the time—to keep Bonnie happy because she fucked him so good. He felt Deanna reaching into his house shorts, nails digging when he didn't answer. She was looking at him, playfully appalled.

"You saying Bonnie did Clyde better than I do you?"

"No," he said. "But I don't think she was rough with him like that either, with the nails."

7

George walked into the Green Machine at Spadina and Queen. Pretended to do some banking, sliding the plastic envelope into the card slot. Trap set, he left.

From the north side, Deanna followed Nick Torrence into the kiosk. Torrence smelled cocoa butter, looking over his shoulder. She was wearing the glasses again. Mousy brown hair, Barbra Streisand cut. Open-toe heels, a pastel blue slip under a Lee jacket. Standing close.

"See something you like?" Torrence said.

"Why can't I look? You don't even know you're good-looking."

Torrence pursed his lips. "I'm a retiree."

She stabbed a playful index. "That outfit would make a great bikini."

Torrence turned back. Feeling aware of his purple golf shirt with white palms and matching hat, he ran his thumb along the card slot, removing the plastic envelope. "I saw the report." Facing her again. "Here's your problem. The sleeve has a little fold that you need to grab onto to remove it. That's what the TV said, flaw in your system. TV said I'd be able to feel the fold if I ran my hand over the slot. Low and behold." He held the transparent envelope up to the light as if something might be inside. "TV also said Crime Stoppers is offering a reward."

Pulling up at the corner, George saw the exchange taking too long. He didn't think it had gone bad until he realized Torrence was looking back at him, in the eyes, when Deanna reached into her white vinyl purse, removing a tiny black canister with yellow labeling. It hadn't come to that since Niagara Falls.

8

Bad enough about Killean Jones. Now Cecil was looking at the editorial page, a cartoon portraying a cop, arrows pointing to a hidden pocket.

"Gonna bust that bitch's ass." He wondered if the coffee was making it worse. "Bust that ass."

"There are two of them," Alex said.

"She's the one made a fool out of me. Still making a fool out of me. 'Hidden Pocket Bolan.' Whole city's repeating all-news, all-the-time."

Alex made like he was trying to wipe the smile off his face. "Indeed, heard folks calling in from their cars on the drive in. Now maybe you see why I'm happy about the man on the radio's not talking about me in the first place."

"Bust that bitch's ass."

"You don't even know if this woman is a Windsor Withholder. She pepper-sprayed a man, yes. Might have been, hmm, that the man pulled out his pecker or something. Lot of women carry the spray on account of pecker-pullers. There's that, plus their descriptions don't match."

"He said he pulled the plastic sleeve out of the card slot, just like on the TV."

"Pecker-puller liable to say anything. Besides, they didn't find a plastic sleeve, just like on TV. You need to be objective, junior. Two sides to every story and you only heard one."

"She probably took it. A pro, like you said. Anyway, if that guy whipped out his dick, why would she run?"

"Cecil, you know a woman who wants to be around to deal with that? Questions, trouble. Listen, maybe it was your Windsor Withholders. Sounds like it could very well be a little street justice, too. We don't know yet is all I'm saying."

"Street justice? She pepper-sprayed the poor bastard. Nearly blinded him."

"Don't stop you from using it. Why did you pepper-spray Killean Jones anyway? He was co-operating. Gentlemanly, if you consider circumstance. I had to double-cross the man, pose as a customer, so he's mad enough. Then, the way you blasted him. Give him the spray once, tell him you're going to do it again before you do it. If they had tapes on that, he's Hogtown's Rodney King. You—you could have blinded Killean—and if you blinded Killean, no way I would have lied for you. As it is, I'm going to have to lie again."

"I'm trained," Cecil pointed at himself. "Trained to use pepper-spray. This Windsor Withhold broad? I come up against her and she feels the burn like Killean, only double."

"Cecil, you use that shit more often than Jerry Mathers ever said 'Gee Wally.' Pretty soon internal start asking me questions. As for the case, you're taking this a bit, hmm, personal. Besides, we have a make on their car, so long as Torrence isn't a pecker-puller."

9

Deanna kept up the small garden—a plot about nine feet long, two feet wide—outside the coach house. It may as well have been in the alley, just enough off to the side.

At one end she was training morning glories to trace a child-size wheelbarrow. Three dwarf sunflowers bloomed among patches of lemon thyme, basil, and lavender. At the step she had a red hibiscus in a plastic pot that was supposed to look like clay. Today she found a spot for some forget-me-nots, watering soil around the new plants.

Inside, a couple days of ordering in and watching TV had George skittish. He was looking at himself in the mirror, looking for something to happen, deciding to shave. He did the bulk of the job in the shower, cleaned up in the mirror.

"Still look like hell." He said it again, louder so Deanna could hear. "You think it's safe for us to go out? Been in here two days straight. Two days."

Deanna came in, closing the door. "All-news said that Torrence got a pretty good look, George."

"Not me. Not from that far away. No way he knows what you look like, either. Clunky glasses. All that powder on your pretty freckles—no way. You heard they got a good description yet? Last I heard you were thirty-something."

She had her hands on her hips, slightly insulted, like how could anyone think she was thirty-something? "Where do you want to go?"

"Just get my hair cut," he said, pointing off to nowhere in particular. "That place on Parliament I went last time we were in town. Pick up some more Corona."

"Isn't that what crooks usually do after a crime? Get a haircut, buy some beer?"

"I guess."

"'I guess.' Well, that's why you shouldn't do it."

"I look like hell."

She looked at him, brushing his wet bangs back. "Let me cut it for you." Kissing him soft, full on the mouth. "Give you a hundred-dollar rubdown after, full service."

"Don't think so. I want a flat-top, change it up."

"Okay, fine. And George, there's a dozen or so cards in the dash. Clean 'em, wrap 'em in a bag, get rid of 'em."

"Good enough."

Good enough, she thought, grinding her teeth. "Look, I found three of the cards from Niagara Falls in between the seats, so just you do it, George—good enough."

He shook his head, a non-verbal yeah, yeah. "And I forgot to tell you. Your dad called."

"When?"

"Yesterday." He held in a smile, biting his lip. "When you went for beer."

10

Jimmy Ronzini was as particular with George's sideburns as he'd been with the flat-top. Finishing the job, he said the lamb-chops now looked like Italy with the bottom of the boot cut off. "Had to shave off the islands too." Pulling the bib away, admiring both his wit and craft. "You like?"

"I like." George touched his burns playfully, then the flat-top. "Made me into a marine, Jimmy. A marine."

"Kid, you could land a helicopter on that thing." Tipping six with a twenty, George made for the Accord 40 yards away, facing north near Winchester. He noticed two men in a metallic Mercury Cougar pulling in on the west side, facing south. Normally, this wouldn't have been a panic. But they had parked now, stopping and taking parts of two spaces, so George made them for cops.

Committed, head down, he opened the Accord's door. Square key in hand, he hit the ignition in the same motion. Licking his lips when a navy Lincoln station wagon pulled behind the Cougar.

* * *

"That him?" Alex said. "You and Torrence said he had a pony-tail. Caller said he had a ponytail. I say a flat-top drastic for a man fancies a ponytail."

"Just a sec." Cecil stepped out, running across the street, into the barbershop. "That guy just walked out with a flat-top—he have a ponytail when he came in?"

Recalling the tip, Jimmy shook his head. "No. No ponytail. Just a touch-up. I tell customers every two weeks—no more than three—for the flat-top."

"You are a lying bastard." Cecil pointed at Jimmy. "I can see it in your eyes." Now at the floor. "And there's too much hair around your chair. Touch-up, bullshit."

Out the door, Cecil ran to the Cougar as Alex finished a U-turn and jumped in before the car came to a full stop. "Start the car."

"How the fuck do you think the car is moving, Cecil?"

"That's our man. Barber's lying for him, lying to me. Make a note of it."

"You make a note of it," Alex said, passing the Winchester Tavern. "I'm driving the goddamn car." Neither noticed the Lincoln station wagon hanging back.

***

All three cars headed north now, ignoring the 40-kilometer limit. George flashed the signal and ran a yellow, left on Wellesley. Alex would have gunned through the red if he didn't have to stutter-step on account of some old guy on one of those cripple scooters.

Cecil shouted out the window when they shot the gap.

"Get that piece of shit off my street."

Old guy shot the finger, yelling, "Bite me, able-bodied motherfucker."

They were too late to see George pulling a sharp left onto Rose Avenue, parking in front of an all-terrain vehicle. He thought about getting out, running, hiding. Instead, he took a deep breath and held it as the Cougar continued west, the Lincoln station wagon following seconds later.

"How many they got on us?" George said to himself.

Punching the Accord into drive, he drove slowly to the end of Rose, taking another left at Winchester, wondering how he was going to explain this. Crossing back across Parliament, heading east, he thought better of it after making it through the intersection.

11

Deanna sat on a deceptively sturdy cardboard chair made by one of the students. She had one of their textbooks open, something to do with the Prairies. Cold and wet, and nobody seemed very happy about it being cold and wet. She hadn't turned a page for 20 minutes when George came in and knelt in front of her.

"I've thought about it and you're right, baby. We need a new gimmick."

"Something happened," she said.

"No, no. I was just thinking. How about going back to the duplicate cheque gag at the casinos? That's how we started. Deposit the cheque for chips, lose a few grand, cash out. Simple. If they call to verify, the number on the cheque rings your cell."

"Cute gimmick, George, but you get away with it maybe twice until the gaming associations start talking. Aside from that, it rates for a full chapter in next year's casino operating manual."

"How do you know?"

"Dad told me. What else you got?"

"That was my idea." He stood upright, backing away and sinking into the sectional. "Let's hear yours."

Deanna looked at him oddly, her bee-stung lips making a perfect O. "That was my gimmick, George. I brought you in on it."

"I thought that was your dad's gimmick."

Deanna nodded. "Dad helped polish it up, but it was my gimmick, George. At least so far as we're concerned."

"Okay, but it was me making it new again."

"I'm telling you George, that gimmick is like roast beef on the wrong side of good. Leave it alone."

"Fine, okay. But what are we gonna do?"

"You can't press, baby," she said, softer now. Walking over to the ghetto blaster, cueing the Joan Jett tape. "The gimmick just comes to you. Then you test it, refine it. For example, the Windsor Withhold started off as 'shoulder surfing.' I'd peak over their shoulder, get the PIN, then drop a twenty on the floor." She stopped the tape, hit play. "Tell him that he dropped it. When he stooped for the cash, I'd take the card from the machine. Dad perfected it with the plastic envelope. Said it would be safer for me, safer for everyone."

George was busy thinking how Deanna was running out of outfits. Wearing that blue slip like a dress again, she came walking over to him the same time Joan Jett sang about it. Leaning, pulling him up off the floor, kissing his forehead. "We're just going a little stir crazy, baby. It will pass."

"What do we do until then?"

She looked at him, herself, back again. "The song's on."

"So?"

"So bend me over, stupid."

12

George woke up the next morning at 8:29. It was 8:31 before it registered. His socks and boxers had been unrolled, scattered about along with pants, jackets, shirts.

The $4,500 he'd skimmed and hidden in the false bottoms of his clogs was missing. The remaining $22,000 or so in the fake deodorant cans was gone, too. He gave up searching for his keys when the air conditioner went out. "Fuck sakes."

Opening the door, George saw Alex standing in the garden. He held the AC plug with one hand, badge in the other. Behind him, the navy Lincoln station wagon made a pass.

"Now son," Alex said, moving toward George. "You might not see it like this right now, but you actually the lucky one. Unlike my partner, I'm not going to take this, hmm, personal. I recover what's left of the money, I say you cooperated."

George closed his eyes, feeling self-conscious when he realized that he was scratching his balls. Thinking she's gone, then fuck it, scratching some more. "Maybe you'd just take the money."

Alex's jaw locked in an awkward smile. "Maybe I do. Maybe that's what's best for everyone."

"Anyway," George said, "girl took it."

"So it's like that, huh?"

"Like that."

"Well, she's not going to get too far," Alex said. "Cecil dropped me off when we saw the Accord pulling out of here. Some lady from the neighborhood watch made you. And believe me, Cecil's on the case. Gonna bust her ass, personal. The Accord, yours?"

"You saw me in it yesterday."

"Do you own it, legally?"

"Yeah," George said, nodding, looking down. "Clean. Ownership, papers, insurance."

"Bad plates though."

George forced a smile. "Damn kids."

"Yes, well then it don't matter where we find the money. It's in the car, you're double busted on account of it's in your name. But you got something going for you. Keep cooperating, just tell me the girl's name."

"I thought you said—what's his name?—Cecil's going to get her. Bust her ass."

"Cecil might not be the crispiest chip in the bag, but he is going to get her on account of he wants to more than any other reason." Alex looked at the garden, pointing to the blue flowers. "Those just planted?"

"Yesterday." George said.

"That's called foreshadowing." Alex caressed his lips. "Those are forget-me-nots. Means I depart soon. Hence, forget me not. She's not just running. She was planning on running."

George shrugged. "Still doesn't mean I'm going to help you get her. Even if I did, how does that help me?"

"Now look, son. You were one half of the Windsor Withholders. Had a good gimmick. Real good gimmick. Two weeks from now, they'll be writing folks songs about you. I respect that. Also respect a man protecting his woman. Class act. But that one took your money, your car, and I promise to make it hard if you don't give me her name."

George looked into the clear sky, smiling, smelling her on him, cocoa butter. "Folk songs, huh?"

<h2 style="text-align:center">13</h2>

Cecil slid the magnetic cherry onto the Cougar's roof. Pulled the Accord over at Amelia and Sackville, two blocks from the coach house.

"Don't come too fast," he said under his breath.

Approaching, he heard Joan Jett on the car stereo, not such a sweet thing. Looking into the window. She was wearing the lime halter again. "Should have kept your back covered." Chuckling quietly. "So you're a redhead today?"

"Been a redhead longer than Molly Ringwald," Deanna said. Easy, slow. "Almost 10 years longer." Didn't even ask if she did something wrong. But her eyes were a bit red, like she'd been crying.

More likely the cold-hearted bitch has allergies, Cecil thought, snapping his fingers. "License, ownership, insurance."

"Okay, but it's my boyfriend's car, just so you know."

"Paperwork."

Deanna reached for the glove box, opening it, debit cards spilling onto the rubber floor mat.

"So you are my girl. Kindly step out of your car."

"I keep telling you, it's my boyfriend's car."

Cecil waved to himself. "Slowly." He opened the driver's side, right hand on her left forearm, guiding her. With his left, he was reaching for his own canister when the familiar cloud appeared in his face. Tasting the spice. Dropping to his knees, his elbows, scratching asphalt. "I'll bust your fucking ass."

Deanna jumped back in the Accord, seeing a man approach in her rearview, navy Lincoln station wagon parked behind the Cougar.

"We're friends," he said, bending to her window. "Mutual acquaintance, so hear me. You're not thinking—" Deanna trained her canister on him, the man holding his hands up. "Now just hold on. Nine months I've been waiting to catch Cecil Bolan alone. To show you, I'm gonna..." Looking down at his thirteens, kicking Cecil in the ribs "... put it to him once, twice, three times." Taking a break, picking up Cecil's canister. "This your car?"

Deanna shook her head, no.

"Good. Take it to a paid lot, wipe it nice, leave it. Call your father after that. Man arranged everything. Call him, do what he says."

14

From Wellesley Hospital, Alex headed east, right onto Parliament. "So after the girl pepper-sprayed you, Killean Jones picked your pepper-spray up, shot you with it? Yes, and he beat the hell out of you between blasts? That's what you're putting in the report?"

"He was talking about it, saying he was going to knee me in the face, doing it." Cecil fingered the stitches on his lower lip. Eyes bruised, bloodshot, red. "'Gonna blind you two times.' Then he'd do it. And he's not trained. You can't just leave the spout open in someone's face 30 seconds straight."

"I'm not going to say it's not so, but I can't say as I saw that, understand? No one saw it. You sure it wasn't the redhead?"

"She was the one got me the first time. After that, I'm telling you, Killean Jones—"

"Why don't you call your big toe Killean Jones? That way, he'll always be there for you."

"I could hear his voice, goddammit."

The attendant said the woman had paid for the week. That he remembered her like she was just there, her juicy ass. That he called it in after hearing updates on all-news, all-the time. That he called in after they mentioned the G-string.

"And hey." Alex turned to Cecil. "How come you never said anything about the G riding high?"

"What the fuck?" Cecil said, squinting until it hurt. "What good would that have done?"

Alex raised his brow. "Would have given me a little thrill, reason enough."

"There," Cecil said, pointing. The welts on his face looked worse when the sun hit him. "Far corner, next to the PT Cruiser."

Alex took the closest spot, flicked off the ignition, pulled a clothes hanger from under his front seat.

"I think that old redhead girl's just plain difficult," he said. Getting out, crossing the lot. "Expect that heap to be wiped and locked."

Cecil in tow, Alex approached the passenger side. "Good sensible car. Smart." He was working the hanger through the window, looping it around the inside latch.

"Sometimes I wonder who's side you're on," Cecil said.

"Sometimes I wonder myself."

"Sometimes a lot of people wonder."

Alex looked up, shielding the sun. "Cecil, I keep telling you you've got to bring yourself to think like them. Good scammers, I'm the first one to tip my hat on account of they teach me something before I bust 'em."

"Yeah, what can this one teach me? This George, he's so smart."

"Discipline," Alex said. "Discipline enough to know he was wrong about something, even if he wasn't sure what he was wrong about."

"Discipline," Cecil spat. "She left him pussy-whipped, got away, and that means you didn't fucking bust 'em. You only got the one."

"Goddammit Cecil, just take the lesson. I got my man."

"He give her up yet?"

"Not last I heard," Alex said. "And someone already hired him a good, solid criminal lawyer—Derry Hiller's in there demanding bail and such shite. Make Alex say hmm. Somebody loves him." Pulling the hanger with a twist, Alex was in. Cecil tapping on the driver's side. "Just a sec."

Alex riffled through debit cards from the floor, stopping at one in particular, the one with the credit union label, reading the signature on the back, smiling. He opened the driver's side door and Cecil got in, sitting next to him. Punching the eject button on the stereo, he took the tape and said Joan Jett. Trying to crush it with his hands. Giving up, throwing it into the parking lot, he looked back at Alex.

"Something funny?"

"I just didn't know your middle name was Milroy." Alex held the card like a cigarette. "Cecil Milroy Bolan." Pulling it away when Cecil grabbed at it. "No wonder you so angry."

A Safe Existence on the Outskirts of Town

They had spent the past two hours conspiring and laughing and carrying on at a bar called Steve's Place. Then one of the jokes hit too close to home—something about her kids calling him Daddy. That freaked her out. It sent chemicals associated with grief and guilt and recrimination rushing through her pleasure centers. The terror was returning, swiftly this time, and she was worrying aloud, wondering how the hell they were getting away with it.

That's when they decided to end it.

Right there, they decided to end it again.

"We're merely running high on the new intensity of our brief relationship," she told him, speaking in a tone that sounded so automatic. "I mean, we've barely discovered each other's idiosyncrasies. And there are way too many other factors to consider. None of this is real."

"I know." He looked down because he felt he should. "It's time to go. Time to stop denying our ordinary lives. Time to go home."

"I think it's best," she said, looking at her bare legs.

"Me, too."

That's what they said.

They actually said things like that, dutifully repeating safe warnings they had memorized. These mantras came from a pocketbook she'd been forcing him to read during his lunch breaks. It was called *How To Have An Affair and NOT Get Caught!*

*****

She had a husband to think about, a guy named Gil who sold used office furniture on Plymouth Road. Gil, he made most of the money and took care of matters mundane. She made a bit of money on the side herself doing data entry from home and took care of other matters mundane.

This was in addition to preparing elaborate meals that were cooked to perfection and garnished with herbs from her garden. She was always making the little things right.

Back in Southfield, people on Karl Drive knew her as the mother who could make a geography text sparkle by reading with just the right accent. Such attention to detail showed during report-card time when her children were easy to spot by the gold stars pasted to their foreheads.

The charade, however, had become too much as of late, and the first cracks began to appear when her youngest was caught doing terrible things to a raccoon with common household utensils—something about too much sugar on Saturday mornings, neglect.

More importantly, however, was the tryst itself.

It was the eighth time in 12 years she'd stepped out—the ninth if she counted her brief fling with Agnes Martinez, formerly of Bronson Crescent.

She was a seasoned infidel now, so she recognized the familiar warning signs—the paranoia, the ensuing anger, the way she was forever overcompensating—and she could see the whole thing spinning out of control.

Her husband, her parents, her relatives, they should've seen this coming. Fine, she kept her boys' elbows off the kitchen table, good enough, but everyone remembered the way she was before— back when she fancied herself something of a concert-T-shirt-wearing, rock-and-roll-listening, drug slut. At least that's the impression one should've come away with after reading the tawdry scrawl in her later Cass Tech annuals. And so what? She was proud to have fellated Iggy Pop's thumb from the front row of the Royal Oak Music Theater back in '81. Like, that should've been in the plus column.

None of this could have been lost on Gil, either. He knew her when The Romantics were just starting to break through. Gil, he was the roadie who escorted her backstage after the Masonic Temple gig in '83, and he used to be a bit wild himself, at least until he found God in rehab. Gil had a fucking pompadour back then, so he must have been up to something at some point. For he, too, should have seen that beneath her poised exterior she still felt a vague kinship with the belly dancers he used to take her to see in Greektown.

Gil had changed, man.

He'd cleaned up, and then his hair began falling out. She had reasoned it out long ago and made all the considerations. The only choice was to live her real life on the sly. Trouble was, every unguarded moment became a dirty little secret, just like the gypsy card reader who predicted her future and the doctor who prescribed her meds.

She didn't know the living would be this awful, this average—she couldn't have—so while Gil was hawking three-legged stools from his portable sales center that summer, she was, understandably, ripping through that *How To Have An Affair…* book all over again. Thought of it as a refresher course, and in just a few afternoons she relearned everything. She was thinking ahead, making certain to avoid the common traps, scripting easy, foolproof excuses along the way. The book even taught her what to do if she was in danger of getting caught—and much, much more—just as the back cover had promised.

***

Steve was off punching numbers into the jukebox when the voice of Billie Holiday seeped from the speakers singing "God Bless the Child." Up at the bar, she wanted another drink, but Steve was still agonizing over his next selection like he didn't have access to the locked change container. Her co-conspirator wasn't much good to her, either. He was just sitting there on his stool, thinking about his wife, Beverly, and trying to get his story straight.

"It's her job." He slapped the table with an open palm. "Always the goddamn job sucking the life out of her."

Steve moved back behind the bar, nodding sympathetically on the way. He said, "Yeah."

"I mean," he continued, looking at Steve, "if I couldn't have sex, I'd be out shooting people on the I-75."

Steve kept nodding. Again, he said, "Yeah."

Beverly was a massage therapist who comforted the catastrophically ill. She was a proponent of preventative medicine and preached the therapeutic values of vigorous physical activity. Off the job, however, she required silence and tranquility—more and more all the time now—as if she'd been taking on the maladies of those she treated.

She knew her husband was a relatively decent guy, if not particularly swift afoot. He'd never done anything like this in their four-point-six years. Flashy nameplate and reserved pinstripes aside, he was simple, really. He needed Beverly to wear trashy outfits and talk dirty every once in a while, let him spank her. That was his only real kink. Aside from such soft perversions, he'd been sensitive to her needs, even too sensitive, but easy to maintain.

Beverly also knew he was out there risking everything with some strange woman when he should've been playing squash at the Y. She just hadn't mentioned it.

The whole thing had all gone to hell over the past year, and Beverly was hardly sitting at home in blissful ignorance. She'd known something ever since she found that stupid book jammed between the car seats. Aside from that, he'd been taking two showers a day, something the good book had clearly red-flagged.

And here he was, drinking Steve's stinky draught, stewing and worrying about who he would name as his squash partner tonight. It was getting harder to lie, let alone speak, and it had been several moments since either of them said anything. Suddenly the introspective one, he mentioned that Beverly hadn't given him so much as a neck rub for months.

"Does this mean I am living or dying?"

That's what he said.

"Am I alive, or am I dead?"

He actually said that, as if it was some sort of brief, soul-filled soliloquy. Consciously or unconsciously, he wanted it to be something like that. He wanted to be outside himself, to unlearn everything, to simply get lost. But he couldn't relax, couldn't get out of his own head, which is why he was always picking at his little history like a kid going after a scab.

"What does it mean? Answer me!"

"Nothing," she told him. "Sometimes it doesn't mean anything."

"I mean, Beverly. What did they do to Beverly?"

Sitting on the stool next to him, she cringed. Not at his questioning thoughts, just the mention of Beverly's name. She didn't like the way it sounded, the way it tasted, and it bothered her to be bothered by this.

"It's like Gil says," she told him coldly, looking into the wall of bottles behind the bar. "Some guys are just unlucky."

He looked at her like he wanted to kill her. "What?"

She pinched the bridge of her nose, thinking, you're really not that stupid, then she said it out loud.

"Why be like that?" he said, doing his best to manage his anger, bottle it. "Why fight over this? Why? Why? Why?"

His whining made her think of the botched kneecap job on that figure skater a few years ago at Cobo Arena. "Same reason I'm all the time baking shit for my fat kids. You let it happen."

"Relax," Steve said, pouring bar shots from an amber bottle with a crooked label, "and drink some of this, man."

***

Steve's Place was smack-dab in the middle of downtown, and they usually met there because no one went downtown anymore. Not at night during the week, not unless you were poor, or dumb, or sentenced by an electronic tracking device.

It wasn't safe, which meant it was safe for them.

There was always plenty of seating at Steve's, too.

A handful of factory and office types had been at the bar earlier. There was some laughing, a bit of cursing, along with the incessant babble about who the Tigers ought to trade in order to shore-up the bullpen. But save for Steve and the two of them, the place was empty now.

They were getting high on the beer, and Steve had poured free shots of root-beer schnapps, as he sometimes would. "This one's off the cuff," he told them. "This one's from the bar…"

What Steve failed to mention was that this schnapps was not selling. It was one of the cheap regional brands—from Port Huron or Flint—and it tasted like the vile blend of sugar and copper it was.

Of course, they drank the shots anyway, because they were free. And whenever free shots were poured, Steve deemed it appropriate to offer compliments to their whiteness.

"It's pleasant when I don't always have to deal with the dark ones."

That's what Steve said.

Steve was white himself, and he wanted more white people to come to his place. That way, he figured, more white people would come and more white people would come.

It would be like the old days.

He'd be able to afford a live blues band.

And then more white people would come.

Such thoughts always made Steve melancholy.

"This town used to be the Paris of the Midwest," he told them. "That's what they used to call it. Now, marble lobbies and French pillars are buried underneath layers of grime and plywood all over town." Steve tended to go on, telling them the same story each time, feeling he had the right. "After all," he reasoned, dragging on a filterless Lucky Strike. "I founded my place before all the people left, back when business was good, always good."

This heady era Steve spoke of was a long, long time ago, indeed—before the riots, before Denny McLain, before Jimmy Hoffa, before Hudson's closed, before the information age…

Downtown was rusted-out now, ruined, just like they had been when they met at a simulated English pub in Southfield. She had stopped in for a bite before the get-together with her group that night. It was a pyramid scam called Women Helping Women. Men were *non grata*, which provided an ironclad alibi whenever she needed one.

He had just finished a discrete dinner meeting—something about a new job prospect with a rival firm in Bloomfield Hills— and ended up behind her in the parking lot. She was fumbling for something in her purse and dumped her change on the pavement, making a joke about how she was always dropping things like that. He noticed the way she moved, caught a glimpse of her garters, and was quick to get down on the ground, doing his part to round up $3.27 in quarters and dimes and nickels and pennies. Helpful.

***

She fidgeted on her barstool, playing with her hair, looking around nervously. It was clear that she was going to leave soon. Sensing this, he tried starting over, offering a few revelations he'd picked up from the handy manual they'd been sharing.

"Every year," he said, his eyes widening, onto something, "millions of Americans have extramarital relationships, some that last 20 years." Then he stopped himself, realizing how she'd take it.

"What?" She was ready to pounce, eager for a clue that might lead to the point he was attempting to make. "How does that help us?"

"It's true," he insisted, scrambling for something that would keep her there just a little longer. "In fact, most Americans will have at least one affair, usually more. Did you know that?"

"Yes," she said, waiting for the hook of it. "And?"

He gestured, talking with his hands. "Well, if more people have affairs than not, then the monogamists are more deviant than the adulterers."

"How's that?"

"Abnormal. I mean, it's not wrong to realize your heart's desire. It's humanist."

"Humanist." She shook her head in savage, exaggerated nods. "Good. Fine. That'll make the boys understand everything. I'll run it by them, see what they say. Stupid. You know, sometimes a little knowledge—"

"Alright." Shoo-shooing her away with a wave of his right hand. "Alright."

"You don't think these kids have the sixth commandment burned into their fucking brains? Humanist?"

"Fine. If you're going to leave, then go. Just go."

"You want me to leave?" She pursed her lips. "Do you?"

"Do whatever you want." He pointed to his spot. "But I'm staying right here." Looking to Steve. "Gimme a grasshopper, mouth tastes like shit."

"Yeah, okay." Steve nodded, turning to his bottles.

"I'll go," she said, raising her brow.

"So you keep telling me."

Her face relaxed and she eased back into her seat. He hadn't begged. That right there impressed her. And what the hell? What difference would it make if she fucked his brains out one more time?

***

It wasn't quite 10:30 when they left the bar. Steve tried pushing one more shot of his nasty liqueur, but both of them were loopy enough. They politely brushed Steve off, stumbling outside, leaning against Steve's wall and looking into each other's eyes. A trash-culture collage of day-glos should have filled the periphery just like any other decent urban American landscape. But their only light came from the half-moon and a row of poorly maintained streetlamps.

His hands were on her hips, hers around his neck.

They were drunkenly staggering on the spot, crying.

She wanted to say something meaningful, but she was too busy trying to devise a clever way of taking back everything she had said.

He wanted to say something meaningful, but he was too busy trying devise a clever way of taking back everything he had said.

At her urging, they did their best to remain rational and polite, then they were quiet. They just stood there, locked in place, swaying and blocking out the sounds around them. Neither seemed to know what to do or what to say.

Eventually, they took on characteristics of actors they'd seen doing this sort of thing in the movies. She heard herself talking like Bardot on a binge, noticing him wincing like a confused Brando when she reminded him about the parameters they'd set in the beginning. He bit down hard, nodding and reluctantly agreeing to deem their relationship nothing more than a haven of safety and danger.

"This is virtual reality, a short-term pilgrimage to good feelings and instant faith."

That was one of the things he felt he had to say. His remembered where he'd read it, too.

"It's all about the trust we no longer know at home."

And that was one of her better lines. She'd heard a phone-in guest say the same thing on J.P. McCarthy's radio show earlier that summer.

Breaking it off was the honorable thing to do. Even if they didn't mean to do more than discuss the notion, it had been decided. With a desolate goodbye, they would fade back into a safe existence on the outskirts of town.

***

They were still there five minutes later. He was sobbing and tears were ruining her mascara. She leaned over to kiss him goodbye, except the kiss didn't break. She had him pushed up against the wall's dirty white bricks, her tongue rolling with his. Sticky sweet liquor fumes flared from their nostrils. His hands ran into her white muscle shirt and up the sides of her torso. When she didn't stop him, he carefully cupped her small breasts, gently at first, then gave both nipples an abrupt, harsh twist. At that, her right heel pumped up and down on the cracked concrete as if she was keeping time to a heavy beat.

It was too warm for late September, but she shivered anyway whenever he proved skillful enough to find the spot, for polite effect whenever he lost it. She was smiling fully when he slowed down to look at her in the streetlights. Even her chipped front tooth turned him on.

Violently, she was back on him. Her tongue was in his ear. It tickled, or something. Christ, it did more than tickle. It swished grotesquely in his brain like a jelly fish kicking a habit; its spears searing into his insides. He couldn't stand it if she kept on like that—the noise alone making him crazy—but he didn't want her to stop, either.

That whole time, with a strange woman on him like that, he found himself wishing that he'd stuck with exercise program he began in the winter. He hadn't, of course, but he still had all that good dark hair, and poor Gil—he'd seen pictures in the car, and Gil only had a few wiry clumps of what appeared to be pubic hair stapled to his scalp. Why didn't he just shave that shit off? He couldn't picture Gil with a pompadour, which left him wondering if Gil's misspent youth was another one of her elaborate fictions.

"Is it good?" she whispered, laughter cracking her voice.

At least he thought it was laughter.

He looked into her eyes with an expression that quickly became too serious. "Fuck, I love you." His lips were trembling, making the words come out uncomfortably.

She didn't stop what she was doing, but she didn't repeat his dreaded phrase with a "too" carelessly tagged onto the end, either. The hell had he said it for anyway? He didn't love her, and she didn't love him. It was just that, before each other, they were living purposeless lives, counting down, looking forward to purposeless deaths, and there wasn't a quick and dirty psycho phrase to capture the insanity of all that. They were giving in again.

✳✳✳

Sirens blared in the distance then faded. She was yanking on his belt, reaching down into his chinos and working him until he got hard. His pants began falling, gathering around his leather sandals. Her button-fly cutoffs were undone, too, suspended at mid-thigh. They were jacking each other off beneath a sputtering streetlamp on East Congress near Woodward Avenue.

She looked over his shoulder when a movement inside of Steve's Place caught her attention. Her eyes focused and refocused to be sure of what she thought she was seeing. She felt herself pause as the image was confirmed in her mind. Steve was looking back at her through the screen door.

Her first instinct was to scream, but then she just cackled in short, caustic spurts, kissing her co-conspirator again. He pulled back, grinning impulsively, deciding to take another chance.

"Let's to The Bungalow," he suggested, seemingly silencing the hollow background noise.

She froze, wondering how he could be serious. "At this time of night?"

"Yeah." He nodded. "At the time of night."

"I'm not going to the fucking Bungalow," she said, closing her eyes, thinking about the time. "Not now."

He seemed to be genuinely offended. "Why not?"

She was getting dizzy and held her head in her hands. "It's a school night. Besides, Gil… Gil and… Bonnie? What's her name? Belinda?"

"Beverly," he said.

***

The Bungalow was somewhere else so dangerous it was safe. Miles and miles west on Michigan Avenue, it was a broken adult motel tucked into the poverty suburb of Inkster—a full 25-minute drive from the downtown core. They were considered regulars by then, so the manager would let them rent by the hour.

This was not a place you wanted to be late at night, and you didn't want to be there during normal business hours, either. The area just looked bad enough. In particular, there was a room at The Bungalow where two city coppers had been gunned down by a mother and her two adult sons in the late '80s—something about bad cheques and a stockpile of unregistered weapons. There were claims that Lee Iacocca was somehow involved but said allegation didn't make sense to anyone.

Most of the guests were borders, so the word on 106 had passed through a generation of transient tenancies. The manager behind the bulletproof glass wouldn't even enter that room. Too much bad karma.

The key to 106, however, had been hastily given to them (instead of 109) the first afternoon they checked in. For whatever reasons, none of them good, they insisted on 106 every time, never wondering why it was always available, even when the pink NO VACANCY sign hissed. They never gave the crude plaster-and-paint job a thought, because that's where they tied each other up and had meaningless, brutal sex. That's where they ambled on the sheets, spelling each other's name out loud one minute, only to peek through the blinds to make sure they hadn't been followed the next. It was their room now.

***

"Whatever her name is." She tilted her head back, tired blue-grey eyes playing in the night sky. "I'm not going to The Bunga-low."

He sighed, feeling an obscure sense of jealousy toward Gil, then muttered, "You want to go home?"

She stopped stargazing, looking at him in her tipsy trance. "It's time."

"C'mon." He touched her, sliding the cut-offs past her knees and down to her untied PF Flyers. "Let's go."

She sighed, her face tense. "No."

"You sure?" He thought she was going to cry.

"No... I mean, yes, I'm sure... Christ sakes."

He didn't believe her, and he did. He was so turned-on and

turned-around and fucked-up that he didn't know what she was saying, and neither did she.

***

It was past 11 now, and Beverly would be waiting up, pondering the state of things. Maybe she'd cash-out and head for the sun. As for Gil, he was at home fine-toothing another money-making scheme for the boys. They were selling candy bars for the church this time.

"Fuck it," she said, digging her fingernails into his rib cage and smiling wickedly. "Let's do it here."

"Where?" He laughed nervously. "In the street?"

"Yeah." She nodded, pointing to an empty Big Three product gleaming in the moonlight. "On the hood of that car. On the sidewalk. Up against the wall."

Steam poured hard and fast from a nearby manhole cover.

Punk-metal blasted in padded blasts from some nameless project.

There was a bang to the east and his head jerked in search of the sound. Something told him it was a gunshot, but she was sure someone just set off a firecracker.

It was getting so that he couldn't think, then a squad car passed, its occupants never noticing their degenerating state of dress on the drive by. Or maybe the police thought it best not to notice.

"Your wife won't," she said, tugging at his shirt with one hand, his dick with the other. "But I will. Right here, right now."

"No." He pushed her away. "Not here."

"Why?" She looked at him. "Why the fuck not?"

"Just can't." Hiking up his trousers, fumbling with his belt. "We... This is like... I mean—"

Her brow furrowed with the beginnings of anger. "What?" she

said, never bothering to reach for her cutoffs draped over her sneakers. "Like, The Bungalow is a nice place to take a girl, this time of night? It's alright to take me there? I mean, what am I, a crack whore?"

Pretty close, he thought. And what the hell am I doing yelling at a half-naked woman on the sidewalk in this part of town, this time of night. Fuck around, to jail I'm a goin'.

An undoubtedly politically incorrect remark was on the verge of escaping his lips, but he caught himself, waving his hands defensively.

"Look, I'm just a white boy from Royal Oak out here singing redemption songs. Somebody'll kill us, baby. This is like Hell's Kitchen, maybe worse. They'll kill us for fun. And if they don't get us, the police will. Fuck sakes, put your goddamn pants on. You want we should have Gil and Beverly bail us out?"

She was about to lash back, but she stopped herself, too, realizing that her cutoffs had been at her ankles for quite some time now. She seemed to be stunned but then she smirked as though something was occurring, awkwardly kicking out of her shorts and leaving them on the sidewalk next to her. He was baffled and aroused at once. She smiled, reaching for his perfect dimple, touching his chin, pinching it.

"I don't care," she told him, dismissing his worst fears. "This feels too good."

"It feels good," he said, trying to smile back. "Sure, it feels good. An affair can revive your spirit, book does say that. Book also says half the people involved in affairs are eventually found out. We can't risk this. Not out here. Book says——"

She prodded his chest with finger stabs. "I read the fucking book, too, remember?"

"I know." He put his hands up again. "I know."

She pointed at the center of her own chest. "I'm the one who bought it, and I'm the one who highlighted the important parts, and—"

"I know already, I know."

"And now I'm telling you to forget the whole fucking thing, because I still don't care."

He didn't know what to say, so he said nothing for a change.

"I don't care," she said. "Say it. No one will ever talk to you like this again."

He still felt uncomfortable, so he figured it prudent to muddy the situation further, buy some time. "What does that mean, you don't care?"

She tried a softer approach, cooing while her long, tapered fingers danced in all that thick dark hair of his. "C'mon, say it for me. Say it for the other woman, baby."

When that failed to elicit a response, her hands closed in fists, hammering on his chest. She was crying, more hysterical than he'd ever seen her.

"Goddamn you, say the words."

***

Moments of awkward silence ensued. Avoiding her eyes, he stared off blankly into space. She looked over his shoulder and through the window. Steve was still in his place, gazing at her. She looked down at herself, and she knew she should have been embarrassed, or something, but their lives were already buggered up enough. She tried to pretend that Steve wasn't there, rolling her head back to look at the man she was with.

He sensed her eyes on him again and looked to her, oblivious to Steve's wild glare. He didn't want to know where she was going with this I-don't-care business, so he was wondering about trivial matters instead, diverting himself, compartmentalizing, thinking how she was 28 months older than him even though she looked a half decade younger.

Maybe that's got something to do with this whole come-here-go-away thing, he thought, noticing that the highlights in her hair were fading. She was going to need the full treatment real soon.

He was feeling skittish. The eye contact didn't feel right, so he looked away from her, just as he had all night. Torn cardboard boxes and wonky wooden crates were piled on top of each other on the sidewalk. Most of the stuffing had oozed out of a discarded couch across the street. Somewhere, someone was screaming about something. He remembered all the talk about pumping money back into the core, but almost every storefront was boarded up. The night buzzed with the wings of tiny insects, then the People Mover rumbled lightly overhead, rolling smoothly on its high-tech track without a passenger, losing more money on the way.

She could see that he was no longer there with her. He was still wearing his practical after-work pants and his sporty powder-blue button-down shirt was still unbuttoned. He needed an XL because he was getting a bit of a gut, and dark circles were gathering beneath his eyes.

He didn't have much time left at being young.

Pictures flashed, which made him feel trapped in his own little movie in his own little head. He saw himself stuffing his pockets with licorice sticks, chocolates, and baseball cards—and he wasn't paying for any of it.

The flashbacks left him thinking of his home in Royal Oak. It was like all the other houses on Marion Road, more or less. It was a house without a face, without expression, without color, muffling the silent screams of a sprawling suburbia from inside. He thought about his wife and wondered what terrible things they had done to end up like this with each other.

Looking off into the cover of night, he watched the Canadian Club sign spelling itself out at Hiram Walker's headquarters across the river in Windsor. The sign was more than a mile away, but the red and green neons were clear, even without his lenses.

"Did you know," he began, whispering, coming slowly down to earth, "that the whiskey sign over there is the biggest neon-light-writing sign in the world. My dad took me on a tour of the distillery when I came of age."

"I don't care," she said quietly, almost smiling.

He closed his eyes and laughed softly, the urgency inside him gone. He was drained, and when he finally slowed himself down and took a few moments, he realized that he wasn't all that terrified. He thought he should've been, but everything was just too far gone.

Right there, in the beautiful Detroit night, he decided that whatever happened next didn't matter, not anymore, and the heel of his hand was rubbing firmly against her thigh when he finally repeated her simple refrain.

"It's alright," he said softly. "I don't care, either."

That's what he said.

He actually said that, like they we reaching some natural conclusion, like they were the last two people on earth.

His eyes were closed and she was whispering warm into his ear, holding him close, wishing they were somewhere else. Over his shoulder, she could see Steve standing in the doorway, still looking at them. He didn't seem to be wearing his pants.

THEATER IN AN EMPTY ROOM:
A ONE ACT PLAY

A piano instrumental drifts through Francis' apartment. If he were home, he would comment on the piece's ability to bring one nearer to a state of higher consciousness. Unencumbered by Francis, his nonsense, or the AC he remembered to flick off, the music continues peacefully.

It is Tuesday, July 8th, according to the newspaper sitting on the hardwood floor—pushing three in the afternoon, according to the plain clock on the beige wall. The phone sitting next to an empty highball rings once, twice, then onto the standard third before the answering machine clicks into gear.

FRANCIS, *his recorded voice replaying self-consciously*: Hello, I am not presently available. Please leave your name, number, and a brief m-m-message at the tone.

Instead of a tone, a mechanical cuckoo cuckoos.

RUSS, *hesitating*: Good morning, Francis… It's been a long time. The reason… I'm very ashamed of myself, you coming to our apartment the day things weren't working normal… That's your… It's Russ Lowell, by the way. Me and Jasmine had… Ahh… Gone a little overboard. We're very ashamed, and I wish to apologize. Now, should you have an opportunity, I was hoping you may phone me, because we're thinking of getting into an in-patient program, and I want your recommendation on whom you feel would… Ahh… Help us to the best of our… It's not just a case of going to court, it's a case of reorganizing our lives and becoming the people we are.

JASMINE, *whispering emphatically in the background*: We are business people.

RUSS: Yes, professionals... We've been very self-destructive, but... Ahh... It wasn't something we chose. It just happened. We're in a position now where we can get into a lucrative clothing bu... Ahh... Importing business. And we must first come to grips with ourselves. We're hoping you can give us some comment on how we can go about it. I know you're the man to do it, because I know where you've been, and I know where you're at, and I know that... You have your head on your shoulders. So, should you get a chance, please phone me at...

JASMINE, *realizing Russ cannot remember*: 525-

RUSS, *picking up the familiar rhythm*: Yes... 525-1649. That's 525-1649. Ahh... In any event, have a nice day, and I hope your son is doing well with your son. Take care.

Russ hangs up, the tape rewinds, and the piano continues playing, fading as the curtain falls.

Thursday, 5:34 a.m.

You didn't sleep well last night, Henson.

You rarely do.

Getting to sleep is always the easy part, but you can't stay with it. Every morning the anxiety kicks in right about now, your body telling you it's time for a cigarette. That's when you wake up for good, staring at the ceiling above your bed, staring until day throws light against the dull stucco, slowly turning it white.

Your teeth ache and your jaw is sore. It's from all the clenching you do in your sleep. The ensuing pains get so bad that you make a brief moaning sound, the noise a slightly wounded animal might make, then you stifle it.

This is your routine. This is the point when you stop praying for another few minutes of sleep to come down. Instead, you're smoking, listening to traffic and sporadic sirens five floors below. Before you get used to the noise pollution outside, the aging club kid next door starts his morning with Special K and the Village People. Every day, it's "YMCA" then "Go West." "YMCA" then "Go West"…

Louder and louder at each turn of his turntable, the happy, happy dance sounds are just as intrusive as real coppers and real construction workers, this time of day. You're simmering in red-hot anger, and it's such a dark lark because you've become the kind of guy who bitches about other people's noise. You used to make your own racket, Henson, a lot of it, back when you were good at eating, sleeping, and your other animal functions.

Before you bought into that new condominium near the corner of Baldwin and Spadina…

Before the transit commission installed new-and-improved warning horns…

If there's good news, it's that fewer pedestrians and cyclists are being killed. You have seen the stats, or at least heard of them.

7:45 a.m.

Cigarettes and coffee offset each other, but only for so long. By the time your tongue tastes itself with distaste the process has gone too far.

You are tired.

You are wired.

Caffeine and nicotine bite through your system like two strays working out territories.

Coughing heavily, you heave, scratching at your sheets. The involuntary refuses to subside so you seek out a needed distraction. Flicking on the radio for company, listening to one progressive rock song blending into another, blending into another, blending into another…

When that fails to console, you stumble into the hallway. Nobody there, so you go ahead and steal *The Sun* from the doorway across the hall. You don't know the woman who lives there, so it's alright. She shouldn't be buying that trash anyway. Just the same, you look both ways to ensure that you haven't been seen by the private police team the board hired to root out people like you.

Safely back in your suite, you flip once to page three, running eyes over Cassandra's white latex outfit—her lovely set of fake plastic tits, a silver belly button-ring with a red bead, and lush heroin eyes. Says here she is 26 with big plans to run her own spa one day. When she's not hanging out with Karizma, whoever that is, the green-eyed Aquarian enjoys movies, dancing, and relaxing in her jacuzzi.

Of course she does, you think. Either that, or she sweats it out every night, grinding to "Ballroom Blitz" at some high-end striptease establishment in the suburbs.

You enjoy none of the things Cassandra gets off on. Time doesn't allow for it, so you sigh, looking at her once more and briefly casting her at the center of one of your fantasies. With that last glance, she's gone forever, because you're flipping, flipping, flipping… Until something on page 21 stops you abruptly, another story about the manager of Food Services, the one who went missing last year. The cafeteria manager from the building you report to every morning at the corner of Bay and Grosvenor.

Tabloid says they found a sleeping bag filled with his skeletal remains on the east side of the Humber River. That part makes you wince, but when you look at his picture you can't place his face. You don't remember the thin moustache, the narrow eyes that were too far apart, the gelled back salt-and-pepper hair…

All of a sudden it doesn't seem so bad. He looks like everyone and no one. Even if you had known him, even if you could place him, you wouldn't be able to care. You're too worried about finding the will to do the things you must do.

8:18 a.m.

Hot water from the shower is soothing, but it's only a Band-Aid remedy. Tension quickly builds in in your chest, tightening as you towel dry.

Too many voices speak in monotone.

Too many people live in your building.

Downstairs the congested street is getting meaner and louder and faster.

You need something to slow you down, but the doctor won't give you any more. Too many things are happening and you don't know how to string them together.

Looking for one more reason, key words repeat and repeat as you stickhandle a disposable razor—one that you should have disposed of by now—around your trouble spots.

You think it doesn't have to be like this.

And you really believe it.

Every fucking day.

8:38 a.m.

Strangling yourself with a navy-and-cobalt paisley tie, you briefly entertain alternative theories, thinking, maybe it's you.

This philosophy fails to resonate so you nix it, switching back to sobering conspiracy conjecture. Your reactions and contradictions are perfectly natural, given your surroundings. They're making a conscious effort to tire you out, like it's in their best interest that you're all the time manic, like you'll be more productive if your resistance is low.

That's it, you decide, pulling a blue suit jacket onto your torso and cackling at your reflection.

You've done nothing to bring any of this on.

Could be, Henson, but you are still going back for more so you can save up for a new blue suit and a new blue tie, something nice that you can wear to work.

Your half-hearted smile fades in the mirror when you feel the tightness of your old suit.

You are putting on weight. Hairs are growing out of your nose. Your ears, Jesus Christ, look at your ears. Your face seems greyer. Red blotches. Dark circles.

8:50 a.m.

By the time you hit the street there is no denying it anymore. You are late, again, run-walking eastbound through the university campus. This is not the carefree stroll you imagined when they brought you in seven and a half years ago.

They are cutting back now.

Firing you would make the populace happy, at least that's what the polls say. And, according to the papers, those polls are accurate 19 times out of 20.

It's a race to the bottom. You know that. You read all about it in the Career Section, so you have been working hard, man, and working hard to be seen working hard. You have stomach pains and you're stumbling—stumbling through the crucial stumble of the trivial, getting later as you get closer.

You are a Project Office Coordinator with the Ministry, whatever the hell that is. Now that you think about it, you don't know what it is that you do, exactly. The only thing you are sure of is that you write something they call Contentious Issue Reports. These reports need to be typed into your computer. The Ministry has provided a specially designed program that allows you to properly format said reports. This way, they can be printed and placed in a binder so that the Minister can easily refer to them when such issues come up during Question Period. Beyond that, you don't know who these reports end up with, other than the Action Man. He doesn't think to tell you about further distribution, and you don't dare ask.

Your co-worker Taso has a theory. He thinks the Action Man leaks your documents to select private interests. But you believe they would have caught the Action Man during the witch hunt, if in fact Taso's wild allegations were true. The Ministry, as you know, has people in place with ways of following such paper trails. Powerful computers, the newsletter said.

Like you, Taso used to be an Office Project Coordinator, too. Unlike you, he was promoted to a Director (Acting) in the Strategic Planning Branch. He works on the tenth floor for now, one floor above you. And Taso, he is pretty sure they are testing him.

"They want to see if I can succeed with special assignments requiring detailed organization."

Taso actually said that. He might've even meant it.

You don't feel as though you can succeed because you can't bring yourself to care. You don't want it bad enough anymore. That's what has you worried. You are burnt.

A few blocks from work, you get this image of the Action Man in your head. He is in his office, watching your empty cubicle, tapping his spit-polished oxblood brogue on the tiles for every second you are late.

He'll have the feedback on your desk from the report you've been working on.

Eleven Ministry people are being consulted.

Today, you will go through 11 sets of omissions and revisions before it goes back to the same 11 people. Then you will make fresh copies of a shorter version, and they will make more omissions and revisions, some of which will be contradictory. This will cause fights among the 11 truth makers, leaving you caught in their bitterly personal crossfire. Nonetheless, this document will keep going back to them again and again and again, shrinking each time. At some point, the truth makers will work it out and the report will stop returning to your station. You will never see it again. In fact, if the report is contentious enough, you will never even hear about it again.

Meanwhile, you're still walking.

The tie is strangling you.

You feel the extra starch they put in your shirt, always too much starch.

Sweat is dripping off your brow.

You are the oldest young man on earth.

9:10 a.m.

Briefly, you entertain the notion of clothes-lining a cyclist riding toward you on the sidewalk. Realizing this is inappropriate, you stop yourself in time, turning your attention to the women in cotton dresses and sneakers and lipstick. These women are pushing towards your building in a determined manner known as the Pep-Step. You enjoy the way that they move.

Albeit more labored, you walk right along with these women, worried that they are aware of your primitive desires and ill-informed opinions. You organize these guarded secrets in your head as you pass the peaceful protesters. In unison, they seemingly chant just for you:

Hey hey
Ho ho
The government of the day
Has got to go
Hey hey
Ho ho…

The government has changed hands three times since you started, but it's always the same people chanting the same chant. It makes you wonder how anyone around here could be peaceful—how anyone around here could want to be peaceful—then it's through the revolving glass doors.

You see co-workers you have never met and never will. They pace in front of the elevator with tight, faceless faces, waiting to limp into cubicles that may forever define them.

This is the time of the day when your stomach pains throb like the ripe ulcers they are maturing into, the time when you are most terrified.

Whatever brings you to this place, you dress the same as everyone here because you must.

You think the same.

Life is just easier that way.

You talk the same.

I can't see the difference. Can you see the difference?

Just like Madge, you're soaking in it, Henson, and, in all like-lihood, you pleasure your pleasure zones in the same manner, making the same simulated faces, the ones you learned from the used magazines you secretly buy on Yonge Street. The others buy these recycled magazines, too. And yes, they feel shame for they have also been educated.

A framed map in the hallways reads: YOU ARE HERE.

The urge to weep overwhelms you, but you cannot follow through on that urge, certainly not here, not now as the security cameras roll, not as the Special Constables look on from several nearby perches. You can only stand there, wondering how it is that the Special Constables represent any threat to you. They don't, after all, carry weapons, except for their big black nightsticks. Besides, Henson, you're no killer. And the Special Constables, they're just glorified security guards.

The bell next to one of the boxcars chimes.

A skyward arrow turns green as the doors open.

It's everyone for themselves, all jockeying for personal positions and happy places.

Bouncy elevator music invades your senses, "The Love Boat" theme, along with the naturally manufactured scents of other animals. When your eyes meet those of a beautiful woman with bubblegum-pink lips, both of you think blow job and look away.

The doors are just about closed when stubby fingers pry them apart from the other side. A shiny bald head is exposed as the twin chrome doors continue parting. Brilliant white teeth smile, hallmarking your dental plan. Round and silent, the face before you wears horn-rimmed glasses. A blue suit two cuts above yours covers the pear-shaped body. A flat-blue tie hangs over the belly. His white shirt is crisply starched, but not so badly as yours.

The man is a Regional Program Director.

That's his hard-fought-and-won title, but you secretly refer to him as the Action Man.

He is the main reason you can't get paper off your desk.

You sense the Action Man sensing you as he continues holding the doors ajar, herding people into the box as if they are his people—maybe they are—and, after all that, he lights up the No. 2 button.

A secret voice screams, echoing through your insides like a howitzer.

I HATE YOU I HATE YOU I HATE YOU…

The Action Man looks at you like he can hear your secret voice. With one brow raised over the frame of his glasses, he nods and says, "Henson."

You nod back. "Mr. Skinner."

Then you look down, the voice in your head slowing, subduing your string of foiled rage.

i hate you i hate you i hate you…

10:42 a.m.

You meeting starts late. Such gatherings always do. They intended to keep you waiting. That was part of the plan.

The hook of it is someone in your department has ignored the hierarchy again. This time it was Kelli. She's known to burn off extra calories by taking the stairs. Up until now they have spoken highly of her. She's cute and hip (but not too much so). She wears the correct outfits, the correct color—the color of the party in power—and she smiles pretty for the Action Man. She gets her work done on time and respects the notion of doing more with less during these times of fiscal restraint.

Like you, Kelli is a Project Office Coordinator.

Unlike you, she had an idea, and sent an email directly to the Minister, who, out of habit, initially denied all knowledge of said email. That was before the Minister flip-flopped—as she is prone to do whenever new polling information becomes available—and introduced the idea to Parliament as a way of channeling capital into a handful of her pet causes.

Inside, you're chuckling quietly. It's not that you're a bag of hammers, Henson, not at all, just that you know better than to take that kind of initiative. It's better to simply lay low and cover your ass. Still, you're stuck sitting there at that round table while Ms. Reid, the middle manager type, drones on over the irregularity of Kelli's actions. Seems Kelli's email has sparked an internal investigation. Security now needs to be checked and re-checked.

"Mr. Skinner and I have taken great pains in reminding this department about protocol," Ms. Reid says.

At that, you sigh. The repetition of this message is getting to be a bit much, you know that, but then Ms. Reid is looking into your eyes, pursing and moving on only when she is satisfied that you fear her.

"You are all aware of the fanatical pecking order," she says. "Our directives as per the chain-of-command have always been clear…"

You nod automatically, thinking, *yes, we have to work harder than you.*

The Action Man stands next to Ms. Reid, crossing his arms knowingly, taking his cue, speaking his words to form a clear demonstration of his solidarity with Ms. Reid and their front against you and you and you…

"People," he begins. "This cyber breakdown is so unsettling that the issue has been prioritized on the agenda for the next Departmental Management Committee Meeting."

They talk to you that way every day and you still don't get it. Sometimes, you find yourself talking to your alter ego in the same manner.

11:40 a.m.

Clears shafts of light shoot through a window, lasering ultraviolet into your cubicle. You are still sipping coffee even though it tastes like thin tar.

Stale air circulates and recirculates.

You feel nervous, mean.

Nicotine withdrawal takes full effect while you deal with the amendments the Action Man has left on your desk. You want to make the revisions before he returns, but there are scores of them. You are also having trouble with some of the new language when the Action Man appears, walking by your cubicle and looking into your space. He knows that unhappy employees are more productive. He has seen the case studies.

Moments Past Noon

"La Bamba" by Ritchie Valens plays in the background, just like last Mexican Day. As you did yesterday and the day before, you meet Taso. The two of you wait in line, talking shop and carefully considering today's specials.

"They're going ahead and selling off the rest of Hydro," Taso says. "I've always been against it, but—"

"Yeah, yeah." You wave at him dismissively. "Like the private sector has its shit in a pile." Pointing at the menu 10 feet above. "What are you having?"

Taso doesn't answer right away. The two of you just stand there, getting a look at what everyone else is eating. While most of it seems to look like food—with a possible exception being the tostadas—Taso wonders why you put yourself through this.

"Only the clubhouse is safe, Henson. You know that."

Problem is, Jennifer is in charge of making the clubhouse. You know her as Jennifer because she wears a red-and-white nametag identifying her as a Food Services Preparer. The two of you share little dialogue, despite the fact that she has made your lunch for seven and a half years.

Jennifer is known for her courtesy. Understandably, this upsets you. She is sinister—somehow, you just know that—and she wears the same stunned look every day. Your paranoia feeds off this costume expression of hers. It makes you feel unsure, so you look to Taso. He looks away, knowing what's coming.

"She's stupid," you whisper. "Stupid like Columbo. Sure, with the peak of her Food Services baseball cap turned up, she may not look like she's splitting many atoms, that's—"

"Right, Henson," Taos sniffs, confident that any petty conspiracy would be logistically impossible in such a place. "That's her angle, and the pristine beauty here is that only the two of you know she is fucking with you. Ever mention this to your therapist?"

Your head nods in jerks. Watching Jennifer, you note that her bib is too tight, outlining her breasts. Red polyester pants run up the crack of her ass, frightening and arousing you at once.

Brace yourself, Henson, a voice inside says. Be careful.

"A club on brown," you tell her. Hoping against hope that today will be different. "With fries, and to stay."

Jennifer stares through your forehead, smiling, nodding, and slapping pieces of sandwich together with slices of white you begged off on. "You want that on brown or white?" she wonders aloud, even though it's too late.

"Brown," you say, feeling a familiar fear burn. "With fries and to stay."

She smiles like a poised praying mantis. "Fries?"

You pinch the bridge of your nose, closing your eyes. *Every fucking day. What part is she having trouble with? What? What? Her only joy comes from fucking with me?*

You know the answer to these questions.

You also know that your child within is about to snap and scream, outwardly this time.

"I want my club on brown," you tell her, pointing with your index. Jennifer continues garnishing the white sandwich loaf with mayo and alfalfa and tomato. The futility becomes more than you can handle and you end up losing your mind for a few seconds, almost screaming, "WITH FRIES, TO STAY, WITH BROWN AND ON FRIES… AND I'LL TELL YOU SOMETHING ELSE: I WANT IT ALL TO GO. I mean, TO STAY, ALL OF IT."

You have expressed yourself, Henson, but since you haven't done so for a number of months, it all came out. You talked too much and you went too far. By the end, you didn't even know what you were saying anymore.

With the cafeteria line in ghostly silence, the tape deck clicks into auto reverse.

"Guantanamera" seeps out of the distorted speakers. Considering that it's Mexican day, you try to change the subject, noting that "Guantanamera" is a Cuban song, inappropriate as such.

Taso gives you a sour laugh, shaking his head and taking two steps to the right.

People stare.

Whispers run through the room like poison darts.

Someone says you are adulting poorly.

Looking back at Jennifer, you see the short-order ogre's mouth hanging open. Her grey-blue eyes are without luster. She smiles slightly when she gets a bead on your line of sight.

She got you last.

She got you last again, man.

You used to worry that she was going to erupt and throw food at you, but that woman just calmly dumps your slop into a Styrofoam container. Scribbling the contents in black marker on the outside, she pushes your food across the counter and at you. That's when you pick it up and walk away quietly, taking your rightful place in line, taking inventory of your household weaponry, waiting as your fries get cold.

Minutes later you pay $4.23 and they let you go sit with other workers eating their own cold food.

"Bad move, Henson," Taso tells you with a deliberate shake. "You're on your own today." He picks up his clubhouse, leaving the plastic tray behind and walking to another table.

You do not risk a rebuttal because you need Taso.

Lunch is already half over.

1:05 p.m.

A neon-pink flyer sits at the top of your mail tray, chock full of information on the Minister's upcoming fundraiser.

One-hundred dollars a plate, as you expected.

What with your condo fees, you cannot afford this. But ignoring the Minister's partisan communiqué would be seen as a slap in the face, whereas simply purchasing a ticket would make do as a solid demonstration of your loyalty. This bit of protocol you are aware of.

The Minister's key staffers will be making a list, and they will remember your support, or lack thereof, when they look at making further cuts to bolster the third phase of their austerity program in the fall, doing more with less.

You conduct a quick postmortem of your lunch-hour disaster, and right away you know how your money should be spent. With this clear, you opt for a high-protein diet until payday, lots of peanut butter, scribbling out a cheque for two plates. Maybe you will take a date, maybe one of those women wearing all that cotton.

1:43 p.m.

You see the eyes of the other workers, the way they stared at you, the way they moved away. You want to go back to cafeteria and tell them something, but you're not quite sure what that is. It doesn't matter. They're all at their assigned stations now, and you're sitting in your cubicle, gulping more coffee, trying not to think. Dammit, you are trying hard.

The Minister's office now requires that report by morning. Every time you start making changes, your mind drifts away from the scribble and over to Jennifer… Your run-in today… Brutal sex acts… The high cost of living.

You'll have to work late, and you resign yourself to this the moment before Taso calls. Now he wants to talk to you, because he has a scoop—a great big fucking scoop—and he just can't keep his mouth shut. Taso tells you that the police came to arrest Jennifer after lunch. He goes, "It's on the radio and everything. They think she killed the cafeteria-manager guy, the one who went missing."

You go, "The one in the paper?"

"Yes, Henson, Why? What other one could it be?"

Taso is on the verge of seething, so you pull back.

"I don't know," you tell him, pounding your desk. "Just wanted to be sure, is all."

Taso's patience wanes. "Listen, fuck. They went over the bones in the sleeping bag, and they figure she shot him right in the face three times: BLAM BLAM BLAM BLAM."

"That's four BLAMS."

Taso tells you to shut-up, that the number of BLAMS isn't relevant. There are details, he says, teasing. "Don't you want the details?"

You want the promised minutiae, so you remain obediently quiet, listening politely and doing your best to work yourself back into the loop. Problem is, Taso enjoys the new recognition he receives, so you wonder if his details are intentionally fuzzy. He can't quite tell you why they think it was Jennifer—or much else for that matter—only that they've taken her away.

It doesn't matter, you decide. Someone finally got to her. That's the important thing, the only thing that matters.

Exhaling like you would at sexual climax, you feel the urge to smoke in your non-smoking environs, which, nonetheless, continue killing you slowly with other assorted toxins.

"I've outlasted her," you whisper calmly.

It doesn't bother you that Taso's report is long on speculation and short on details. He's still going on and on, and you're not listening, at least not until there is a change in Taso's voice, leading you to sense someone of importance, maybe the Action Man, invading his personal space. In the next moment, he has to go.

Relief continues flooding your insides, soothing exposed nerves like only the white pills could. Instead of spreading the word to co-workers in other cubicles, you allow yourself several minutes of selfish bliss.

You are thinking clearly for the first time in months.

Turn on your transistor and sure enough Taso's good to his word. But the radio doesn't have much in the way of details either—just a news brief, then more reports of cutbacks. Still, it's confirmation, and good news travels fast. People in other cubicles are gabbing wildly into their phones and sending trashy emails. You never send trashy emails because they have been checking up on that sort of thing with their powerful computers.

2:41 p.m.

Downstairs, you join Taso for a cigarette. A few other Ministry people are having a meet out there as well, theorizing and eulogizing like tape recorders.

Leah, for one, goes on about how efficient Jennifer was, waxing in pre-programmed melancholy. "She could always recite the menu with full calorie counts."

Clarence agrees. "She was so self-efficient," he says. "But she did maintain a social distance. Probably had a shitty childhood. Felt like she was excluded. I mean, you just don't wake up and decide to kill. Somebody did something awful to her, the poor thing."

Taso rubs his chin, speculating that Jennifer's violent streak had something to do with being alienated from her labor, quoting Marx and Engels.

"Laborers, who must sell themselves piecemeal," Taso says, pausing and widening his eyes, "are a commodity."

Which, of course, makes it perfectly alright to cap your boss, slice him up, and stuff his bits into a bag. I mean, that's okay, right?

But you don't say that. You just nod each time one of them says something or nothing. Sucking on a cigarette in the shade, you are rushing to finish smoking and talking. It's too hot, muggy. That makes you stubborn, sluggish. You want to know what made Jennifer snap, and you want to know before recess ends. But these people can't tell you.

Taso is saying something else now, something else he memorized while earning impressive letters at an impressive post-secondary institution.

Once again the diplomat, you're back in the fold, nodding and pretending to consider all points of view. But you're not listening anymore, not really. Not at all. You're too busy smiling, just smiling and thinking about blowing up the building.

It's 11:56 when I hear a cat stubbornly meowing outside my apartment. Hiking up my house shorts, I get out of bed and make for the door, peeling back a piece of tape covering my peephole. I put it there so people can't look in on me.

From my fisheye view, I see the little silver number from the far end of the hall. She is on a sky-blue leash and holding firm to the carpet with her claws. Pulling the other way, her owner, the anti-smoking lady, shushes.

Whatever the anti-smoking lady is doing outside my door with her cat at minutes to midnight, the little silver number continues hanging onto the carpet fibers, wailing. I'm no authority on these things, but I believe she calls to the two tabbies living across the hall. I look on as Natalia Cauzillo opens her door. Holding her blood-red smoking jacket together, she ignores the anti-smoking lady, bending down to say hello to the little silver number. That's when her tabbies escape to do the same.

"Nosey," the anti-smoking lady says, chin nodding to her silver cat.

Natalia stands upright, wrinkling her face, bringing severe bangs closer to her brows. "And yet I can't help but think that the little thing gave you away."

The anti-smoking lady has been at it since last year. It was December when she put a sign on her door demanding that there be no smoking within 50 meters. Although I didn't think it was enforceable—like you can't just type something up, tape it to your door, and declare it law, even in Canada—I knew right away that her missive would put me on the bubble, given that she lives 56 yards south of Natalia's door and mine. I've paced it off but have yet to convert my findings to metric.

Whatever, I haven't seen anyone smoking in the halls since they threw out the poor old lady three doors down and across. She used to fall asleep while she was smoking. And yes, the fire department was involved on a number of occasions. Unless she died, I'm pretty sure they brought her somewhere she can't smoke at all.

As for the anti-smoking lady, her sign was ripped in half before Christmas. The remaining words stood in martyrdom through the holidays until she replaced it with a letter of support from a nearby neighbor, who, apparently, had just spent their first New Year's Eve in downtown Toronto and did not appreciate the array of smokables consumed. Since then, it's been one scrawled warning after another for fellow tenants to stop smoking in their own homes.

From what I understand, smoke had been detected on or about Labor Day, hence four more letters of support, one of which claimed 614 was firing bottle rockets off his balcony, more smoke. Yesterday, I noticed a new communiqué including allegations against unnamed residents revolving around the burning of even more volatile substances.

Now, I can't say for sure that the anti-smoking lady is sniffing under our doors, just that it seems odd to find her there trying to pull her cat in the opposite direction at minutes to midnight on a Friday. I mean, I either can't stop smoking or I won't, but at least it keeps me from lurking around like that.

"Have you been smoking pot?" the anti-smoking lady wants to know.

"Here we go," I whisper to myself.

"I'm burning incense," Natalia says, looking past the anti-smoking lady and at my door.

"Incense?"

"Yes, incense," Natalia says, reconnecting with the anti-smoking lady. "It's called Love. An aphrodisiac."

"But you're alone."

"What's that supposed to mean?"

"It means you've been smoking pot in there," the anti-smoking lady says, pointing her index past Natalia and into 626, then to her own feet. "And you've been smoking tobacco out here."

"First, I've never smoked anything in the hall," Natalia says. "Second, whatever you think I'm doing in here, you've got to be kidding. Get drunk, get a hobby, or get yourself off—I don't care—just get going."

"I can see it in your eyes," the anti-smoking lady says. "You've been smoking pot."

That said, she finally has the little silver number heading south. As they pull away, Natalia says she might as well get her money's worth, seeing as how she's getting the blame anyway, and reaches into her pocket, retrieving a Zippo and a pack of cigarettes from her smoking jacket. She lights one, hits it, blowing smoke after the lady, then shoo-shooing her tabbies inside. Taking a long drag now, she exhales, letting go of a lovely plume in the flickering hallway light. When I hear the anti-smoking lady let herself in 56 yards away, her lock clicking, Natalia takes another hit. Exhaling more dramatically this time, she smiles, focusing on my peephole.

"Are you cold?"

Seconds pass as I cling to my silence.

"I can hear you breathing," she says, still looking. "And it sounds like you're cold."

Scottie Scrivner searched for an appropriate gift fast, plucking a copy of *Casey at Bat* off his bookshelf. It was beat-up, the dust wrapper dog-eared. Aside from dents on all four corners, the insides remained intact. Scrivner thought the old-school illustrations by Christopher Bing made it look vintage, if only it hadn't been for the 1988 publishing date.

Wrapping it in craft paper left over from last year's move, it was decided. Scrivner was going to say that he found the book at an antiquarian shop, Elliot's on Yonge near Wellesley, on his way to the party. That's right, he was going to choose his words carefully. He wouldn't say the book was antiquarian, just that he bought it at an antiquarian bookstore. Casual, like it was an afterthought. And yes, they wrapped the book that way at Elliot's.

Book in hand a little more than an hour later, Scrivner would arrive at Ian Selby's surprise birthday party. As these things go, it was no surprise. Selby himself had been the one to call Scrivner with a late invite. Said he just found out from Redman, his back-up at shortstop, who gave it away by leaving a message for Sabine, Selby's wife, on the couple's voicemail, then Selby picked the message up.

The party was to be outside on the roof deck at Rico Carty's Bar & Grill at Danforth and Main. It used to be that Carty was a designated hitter with the Blue Jays at the end of the '70s. He was listed as an infielder/outfielder, but the Blue Jays never let him do any fielding. At bat, Carty had hall-of-fame type numbers, a career average of .299. In the field, it was said poor Rico couldn't catch a beachball, so it was his hitting that kept him in the game so long.

Now, Carty didn't own the bar & grill bearing his name, and it didn't matter that he had long since left Toronto. Nobody seemed sure of where he was living now, or even the exact arrangement with the bar, though the regulars thought up a thousand different angles, spreading rumors, drunk whispers. Whatever Rico's deal was, the owners used his name to cultivate a very particular clientele, a drinky clientele. And so it was that the bar also sponsored a hardball league for its precise demographic, mostly men over 30 who, like Scrivner, had seen Rico play.

The bar operated the league at a slight loss, but more than made up for it with a natural constituency after games, practices, and during special events. Especially the year-end banquet, which featured an annual speech from Rico, flown in for a week in Toronto. There, it was said, Rico's undisclosed annual business was also settled. But again, a lot of things get said when men past their prime get to playing real baseball and drinking real beer.

Anyway, Scrivner and Selby had become friends—not to mention a solid double-play combo—while playing for the Carlsberg Crows of the Rico Carty Senior Vintage Baseball League.

Scrivner played a real solid second, the glue that held the infield together, according to Selby, even if Scrivner only hit .238 that summer. Slightly weaker in the field, Selby made up for it with a solid .288 at the plate. But sadly, even as they approached middle age, both men failed to understand the crude art of the curve.

While baseball was their common interest, they grew closer after Selby came calling for advice over a divorce. Scrivner was a paralegal who made most of his money serving legal papers to folks who didn't want to be served. Recently re-singled himself, he knew his way around the step-by-step divorce process and handled Selby's matter pro bono.

Selby was out of one marriage and into another now, and the two men they were swapping CDs, DVDs, and books, getting to know each other. They were bonding, Sabine Selby liked to say, though no one else dared put it like that.

***

Arriving alone at Rico Carty's, Scrivner felt the renewed chill. Aside from making brief eye contact with Sabine Selby, it was cold in the physical sense. A half dozen heaters created some buffer. But Scrivner thought that this, being November, was a little late to be hosting a party outside.

Finding a heater and getting under it, he mingled at the bar with Cuyler and Tobias. Then he gave Redman's new Blue Jays jacket a thumbs up, loving the powder blue. There were also four women in a clique Scrivener vaguely remembered, systematically connecting them to some of the other Crows. The blonde in the green cardigan and khakis, the one saying she didn't own any vintage clothing, that was Cuyler's fiancée, Something Figueroa. And the cream-and-coffee colored girl in the brown-leather pilot's jacket, Something Taylor, she was with Tobias. Scrivner was starting to wonder if the redhead was a free agent. Her name was Something McGarvey, Cuyler had said. Scrivner had a habit of remembering only the last names. McGarvey, he thought, making a note of her—a short jean skirt over her leotards and ass, cobalt cashmere sweater, long hair tied back into a naughty ponytail.

Christ sakes, why couldn't Scrivner remember first names? At first, he blamed baseball. Then he figured it had more to do with serving legal papers to people who didn't want to be served, how it didn't come down to their first names until the part where he had to physically find them. That's when their first names came into play. He even made a game of it sometimes, phoning particularly scarce deadbeat dads. Leaving messages on their machines saying they'd won a free TV, where and when to pick it up. Scrivner would break their hearts every time—tickle them with a new TV, then slap 'em with papers. He was smart enough to pull all that off whenever he had to, but he couldn't remember this girl's first name. McGarvey, he thought. He was just going to ask her what her first name was again. And he was going to do it, too, just before he saw Ian Selby in his Montreal Expos hat, waving on his way over.

"Happy—what is it?" Scrivner said. Taking Selby's right hand, pulling him in for a man hug. "Forty-one?"

"Thirty-eight," Selby said. "Now gimme my present."

Scrivner handed the package over. "Found it in an antiquarian book shop on the way over."

"Nice wrapping job," Sabine Selby said, moving in from behind, looking at Scrivner like a gate crasher. "You have one of your queer clients wrap that for you?"

Scrivner pointed at the paper as Selby tore it away, saying that they wrapped it like that at Elliot's. And yeah, he'd expected that the guy who worked there might be queer, so what? Didn't Sabine read the paper? This was Toronto, 2002, and if Sabine didn't like queers, she should probably move to another area-code. Her eyes got big when she saw the book, giving Scrivner a look. "You know why I didn't invite you?"

Scrivner looked at her, then Selby, saying nothing.

"Because it's Dupont's bachelor party down on the second floor," she said. "Didn't want you here upset about Patsy, walking around with that long face of yours at our party."

Selby watched his wife walk away, then began leafing through the book. "She's just mad because you got me something better."

Scrivner pointed his chin at her. "What'd she get you?" Sabine was across the patio now, putting her left arm around the McGarvey girl, whispering in her ear, the two of them looking back. Squinting, Selby smiled without showing teeth, turning to Scrivner. "Bitch got me a facial."

Scrivner shook his head, said he was sorry. Selby said not to worry, that he was going to think of Pam Grier when he woke up with the hangover hornies.

"Give her an extra shot for me," Scrivner said.

Selby looked at him, said yeah, he could do that, but just for the sake of it, not for Scrivner in particular.

That settled, they drank to it, and then they drank along with everyone else. One shooter tasted of both mint and bark. Soon as Scrivner threw it back, he couldn't remember what they called it, probably because somebody else paid for it. He drank some other shooters, too. One was chalky, another milky, yet another smooth and lemony, and the next one didn't seem to have any taste at all. Other than the round of beer, it had been a free ride when Scrivner put his hand on Selby's shoulder, saying it was time to go downstairs and break the seal.

***

Maybe it was just when he was drinking—more like especially when he was drinking—but Scottie Scrivner felt downright claustrophobic when he had to piss in public. It was an intimate thing, and he didn't like kibitzing at the urinals the about the Blue Jays' chances any more than the weather. That's why he was happy to find himself alone until five or six Molson Marlins came barging in, pushing Dupont into the Men's room.

Now, while most of the Marlins were down here on the second floor holding a stag for Dupont, all three floors shared the same john at Rico Carty's. With one of the two fluorescents out, the light wasn't right and Scrivner couldn't see what they were doing to Dupont. Probably trying to fuck 'em, Scrivner thought, doing up his button fly, finding himself pushed up against the corner.

Under normal circumstances, that right there could have been enough to put Scrivner over the edge. But the people from baseball hadn't see that side of him yet—the claustrophobic panic, the pulling at what was left of his prematurely greying hair. That's why Scrivner sucked it up again, calming himself, going to his own personal happy space—St. Marys, Ontario, home of the Canadian

Baseball Hall of Fame—as he tried to push through.

Dupont had missed the previous summer with an assortment of minor injuries to both legs, and he'd been this season's comeback player of the year—hitting five home runs over the 16-game schedule while posting a .307 average.

Guy has all those leg problems, Scrivner thought, and they're literally attaching a bowling ball to his right ankle.

"Fuck sakes," Dupont said. Pulling at the pantleg of his thick coral corduroys to get a better look at the ball and chain. "You want to tighten that?"

They laughed as the Marlin's first baseman—they called him Hoover because he was statistically the worst fielding first baseman in the league—held a key out. "Who wants it?"

"I'll take it," Scrivener said, grabbing the key before Hoover could think it over, tucking it into his pocket the way out. And they just let him through like that, like he was one of Dupont's friends from work. Everybody seemed a little shocked, but not so much as to say anything.

Scrivner hurried away in a steady walk, sensing them all sensing him as he jogged up to the top of the stairs.

"Who is that anyway?" Hoover said.

"One of the Crows, if he's going upstairs," someone said. "Don't worry. They're good guys, the Crows. It's the shortstop's birthday party."

"Not Scottie Scrivner," Dupont said, trying to pick himself up. "Scrivner plays for the Crows, second base. It's not Scrivner with the key, right?"

"No, no," Hoover said. "This guy had glasses."

"Goddamn you, Scrivner's got glasses."

Hoover smiled, thinking what the hell? It wasn't his problem. "Don't worry about it, Dupont. Like I said, this guy had glasses— glasses and a red shirt. Be easy to find when, *if* we decide to cut you loose." Then Hoover turned around, dropping his pants.

Bending over, he placed a Bic lighter between his buttocks, screaming "blue angel" as the flame flickered, singeing his will-knots.

***

Fifteen or 20 minutes later, Hoover came running upstairs like his arse was still on fire. He looked concerned. It was November, man. And dagnabit, people were still yelling at him over that booted ground ball during the play-offs. He was a little loopy, talking slow, looking for the guy in a red shirt and glasses.

"You see a guy dressed like that?" Hoover said. "We saw him come up here."

Tobias, like all the Crows, had been briefed and was now in on the gag. He let the question hang, leaning right as if he might overhear the answer. "When was it you say the man in the red shirt and glasses came running up the stairs? How long ago?"

"I don't know," Hoover said. "Not long. Now come on, Dupont's pissed, we can't get the ball and chain off him. This is serious. Guy's getting married tomorrow, one of our guys. Now who's got that key?"

Tobias looked at Hoover, dropped his head laughing. Said shit, he couldn't remember what happened two minutes ago, he was so fucked on shooters. Who were they looking for again? Guy in a red shirt and glasses, Selby told him. Then Tobias turned to Mankowski, the aging Crows pitcher—51 now, throwing nothing but junk over a league record 11 shutout innings during the second half, striking Hoover out on his old man cheese every time. Had Mankowski seen the man in the red shirt and glasses? No, Mankowski hadn't seen him, either. Neither had Martin, Adams, or Castillo.

Hoover, spotting Scrivner wearing Selby's Expos cap and Redman's Blue Jays jacket, started over. "You're Scottie Scrivner, right?"

Scrivner nodded slowly, yep.

"Little confused about your loyalties," Hoover said, pointing at the cap, then the jacket.

"Hedging my bets," Scrivner said, "just in case."

"Yeah, yeah. Listen, that wasn't you in the loo, was it? Guy that took the key? Dupont's getting madder, man. Can't get that fucking bowling ball off his leg without the key. I think he thinks you got the key, just because of Patsy… Never mind. Like, I don't want to interfere in other people's business. I don't judge, you know. But the poor guy's not taking this well, not well at all, and he's making me ask you. Do you got that key?"

"No." Scrivner shook his head, pointing to his crotch. "Haven't broken the seal yet."

Hoover looked at Scrivner's crotch, then his face. "Huh?"

"I haven't pissed yet. Means I haven't had reason to be in the can yet. Means it can't be me has the key."

"Oh," Hover said. "I didn't think it was you. Guy I handed the key to was dressed a fuck of a lot better than you. What's his name?"

Scrivner made a face, said he didn't know anyone dressed better than him.

Hoover calmed himself, settling into a position where it seemed both arms were cradling an invisible keg. "Look, some guy wearing a red shirt and glasses was holding onto Dupont's key for us."

"Oh," Scrivner said. "You mean, Jiménez?"

Hoover scanned the room. "I don't fucking know."

"Tall," Scrivner said. "about my height?" Waiting for Hoover to nod, okay. "Yeah, Jiménez had on a red Levi's shirt. Glasses. Only wears his contacts during games. Says he doesn't like putting anything into his eyes unless he has to." Looking at Selby. "Was Jiménez wearing his glasses tonight?"

Selby paused to consider the question, nodding. "Yep, Jiménez did have glasses on. Utilitarian working type glasses. He's an electrician. Wears sensible eyewear."

"Yeah, yeah," Hoover said. "Let's rush it along. Where is he now? Like I said, Dupont's sour, man. Talking crazy, like it's my fault."

"Well," Selby said, "is it?"

Hoover, rolling his hand, said, "A little. I gave the key to this guy, Jiménez, even though I didn't know who the fuck he was, so Dupont's on about how that was irresponsible of me."

"Yeah, well then it is your fault," Scrivner said. "Besides, I haven't seen Jiménez for a while." Scanning the room. "Could be he left."

***

Hoover couldn't have been gone 10 minutes when he returned with four other Marlins, all groomsmen, spreading out, covering the room. Hoover came in walking behind everyone like he'd been demoted.

"You see a guy in a red shirt and glasses?" Coles said.

Good and drunk by now, Selby pointed at Scrivner.

Hoover and Coles looked at Scrivner, then back at Selby. Coles pointed at Scriver, saying, "He's wearing an Expos cap and a Blue Jays jacket and Hoover swears Scrivner's been wearing the same combination all night. What's more, Hoover says Scrivner hasn't taken a piss yet, and he's not wearing glasses."

"Contacts," Scrivner said, pointing at his own eyes, thinking how he couldn't see a damn thing. "Must have been Jiménez. Like I told Hoover, he only wears his contacts for games—can't stand putting anything in his eyes longer than nine or 10 innings."

The Marlins repeated the drill a few times, grilling other Crows and their wives—all of whom were playing along—amid worries about how they had to get Dupont to a striptease establishment, The Zanzibar, before last call. Apparently, Sunny Leone was slated to do a special command performance for Dupont at midnight. And, like, the Crows had to pay in advance, a lot, for Sunny to do that special command performance, so they needed the goddamn key—now.

***

First thing Saturday, Scrivner went to the fridge, downing half a quart of low-acid OJ and lighting a cigarette. Placing it in an ashtray lifted from a nearby coffee shop, he went for the white pages, locating the number, dialing. Gary Woods, who appeared in 68 games for the Blue Jays between 1977 and 1978, answered on the second ring.

"Rico Carty's—now we're open for breakfast."

Scrivner exhaled a cloud of smoke, saying, "This is the man in the red shirt."

"And glasses?"

"Yeah, any messages?"

"If you're the arsehole I think you are, there's a guy here plays for the Marlins with a bowling ball on his ankle wants to get married today." Woods was angry, pissed, pounding the bar counter. "The sight of him. Been here all night, you happy? Huh? His fiancée's here, too, crying. Plus, he missed his Sunny Leone show at the Zanzi, and the Marlins paid big money for that. Are you happy now?"

"Just put him on the phone," Scrivner said.

Dupont started talking before he had the receiver to his mouth. Something about how they had checked the Crows roster and there was no such person as Jiménez. "You the right asshole?"

"Might want to try some sugar with that," Scrivner said.

Dupont hesitated. "Scrivner. You got my key or what? You

know I'm supposed to get married today."

"That key is probably worth a lot to you, eh?"

"If you don't bring that key here right now, I'm gonna—"

"Why don't you just call a locksmith?"

"Already tried. It's not that kind of lock."

"Oh," Scrivner said, the eyebrow raise evident in his voice. "That is a very valuable piece of information."

"Why?" said Dupont. "What makes that info so valuable?"

"It makes the key more valuable," Scrivner said. "You're marrying Patsy at what time?"

"Two. Why?"

"How much is it worth to get out of that thing by two?"

"C'mon, man. That's blackmail."

"Hardly," Scrivner said. "I'm a paralegal, know the law, and Hoover asked, 'Who wants it,' the key? He made an offer and I accepted. Given that there was an offer, acceptance, plus the undeniable fact that possession is nine-tenths of the law, I'm pretty much the owner of said key and entitled to charge what the market will bear. Being that it looks antique." Scrivner stopped, picking up his keychain, studying the skeletal design. "I deem it a prize addition to my collection of antiquarian keys. You know how much old keys go for on eBay? Hundreds, Dupont, thousands."

"Goddamit, Scrivner, whichever one of you Crows got that key, joke's over."

Again, Scrivner went over the offer-and-acceptance bit, reminding Dupont he was a paralegal, that this was all a matter of law. That being the case, Scrivner said he was within his rights to profit from said key when most valuable—today, between now and two o'clock.

"Look, I'll give you 50 to get it here, call it a good gag, over," Dupont said. "Just get here with the key."

"I'll do it for a thousand."

"Goddammit, we'll come and get you and take it from you. I'll give you a hundred bucks."

"You don't know where I live, my new address. The league still has me at Patsy's, and she doesn't know where I live now, no reason."

"Look, I'll give you a hundred and fifty. That's it."

"I don't get out of bed for a hundred and fifty," Scrivner said, hanging up.

***

Scrivners's cellphone rang again at 11:17, Dupont calling him this time.

"Got your number off the star-69," he said.

"Are you gloating?" Scrivner made a face. "Price just went up if you're gloating."

"No, no. I'm being respectful, humble. I just wanted to call to say I'm willing to negotiate, settle it in good faith."

"Twelve-hundred," Scrivner said. "Firm."

"Last time you said a thousand."

"It's getting later in the day. I think it's worth more than that now. In fact, every half-hour we get closer to two, it gets more valuable. Then again, I guess the bottom sort of falls out if I still have it after two, calculated risk."

"Look, I'll give you 500," Dupont said. "All I've got."

"Bullshit," Scrivner said. "Don't you have money for a honeymoon? Aren't you taking Patsy on a decent honeymoon? I ought to charge you like 2,400 just for that. Next time you call back you better be ready to take some money out of the honeymoon kitty."

By the time Scrivner was done, Patsy was on the phone. "C'mon Scottie. Don't do this to me. It doesn't have to be like this. It doesn't—" She was still talking when Scrivner hung up again.

He thought about answering when the phone rang a few seconds later. He thought about playing with Dupont a little more before sending the key over in a cab. But he didn't want to risk talking to Patsy—it had been so long—so he just let it ring through. The message light flashed red about 30 seconds later, so he picked up the phone. Hitting the message button, punching in the secret code, then hearing Patsy's voice.

"You know why I left you, Scottie?" she said.

Not yet, Scrivner told himself, waiting a beat.

"Because you think like a criminal."

Clicking the phone off, Scriver slid it across the table, smiling, bringing his hands up to his face. All this time, he figured it had been about something else entirely.

Mom still calls it my rough patch. I had cashed the last of my Unemployment Insurance cheques, my savings account had fallen into the red, and the Canada Savings Bonds Gramps bought me when I was a kid were just about spent.

It was spring. My roommate Geoff had decided to give Alaska one more chance and moved back to Anchorage. I scraped together first and last and rented this postage-stamp bachelor in Kensington Market to cut costs. As for friends, I cut all my ties. I disappeared. I just let myself go.

By early summer, the sun had bleached my hair out. It grew long and straight. I stopped wearing socks in favor of a pair of old sandals, cutoffs, and second-hand T-shirts I found in the market. I was poor. I didn't have any friends. And I was alone.

It's amazing how little you can live on when people don't have your new address—people like collection agents. But money was still tight until I fell into a summer job. I found it through some guy who worked the Seven Seas fish stand where I bought fresh pickerel each week. He put me in touch with a charter-fishing captain named Adrian Rhondo.

Adrian ran a boat called the *Rip Tide*. His previous first mate had quit without notice, so he was pretty desperate. Could be that's why he hired me on the spot, offering four to seven days a week. At $70 a charter, plus tips, it was plenty to see me through the summer. Even though I wasn't much of a sailor, I was comfortable guiding the *Rip Tide* through Lake Ontario after a couple of crash courses. Only when the water got gloomy and mean did Adrian take over. For the most part, he used fish-finder software to locate schools of salmon and barked orders to me up on the flying bridge.

Adrian wasn't like most bosses. He cackled like Satan, promising to get me enough weeks to qualify for UI all over again in the fall. When business was slow, he even loaned me a bit of cash. And once I gained his confidence, Adrian started bringing me on cigarette-smuggling runs to Buffalo.

It was the week before Labor Day when the Cairns Bros. Trucking magnates climbed aboard the *Rip Tide*. Adrian, as he always did with repeat customers, warned me about Terry and Jamey Cairns. *The Toronto Star* was sponsoring this summer-long fishing derby called The Great Salmon Hunt. Writing off the $600 charter as a business expense, the Cairns Bros. were after the $100,000 prize that came with the largest catch.

Lake Ontario was a sheet of amethyst that morning. No white caps, no ripples, no waves. As we left the harbor, a carp broke the glassy water, diving below with a tiny insect, leaving a perfect row of circles behind. Two miles later, we were drifting in a slow troll. The city core, the SkyDome, the CN Tower, and the Gardiner Expressway were enveloped in a green plume of smog, as if a lime rainbow had wrapped itself around downtown. It looked like that every day from the lake. It was almost solid waste. I never knew it was that bad, that it looked that bad, until I worked the *Rip Tide*.

From my perch up on the flying bridge, I looked down to Adrian prepping the last of the six lines we'd be trolling on. He wore a faded Daytona Beach T-shirt with a hooked marlin fighting on the front. The oversized tee was draped over cutoff army shorts and matched his black canvas sneakers. I guessed Adrian to be in his late thirties, but he never talked age, and I never asked. His scalp was nothing but stubble, forever in-between shaves. Adrian's tanned face had been etched and aged into leather by summers of sun and heavy winds. But his eyes didn't fit his surly face. They were filled with the bluest blue, seeming to wax in apology whenever he called out sharp orders. The boat was his home, and the charters were simply an inconvenience he had to deal with to keep it that way.

Adrian told me the same guys would come out every year. They thought they were getting smarter and smarter, but they just made it worse and worse. The lake was clogged with yahoos chasing that brass ring, and the Cairns Bros. were yahoos through and through.

"Keep your course till you're told otherwise," Adrian told me, adopting the stern tone he used in front of customers.

"So Adrian, you been following The Great Salmon Hunt story in *The Star*?" Terry Cairns wondered aloud, flipping open his first can of Coors Light.

"Yes, Mr. Cairns, I know all about our poor man leading the pack in Brampton. By the by, no business of mine, but isn't it a bit early for your grogs? You might want to be recalling that breakfast you and your brother blew all over my deck last summer."

"Not to worry, captain, we got Gravol… I want to talk about going after that big fish. I was reading about that Brampton guy, too, the one who caught the 39-pounder."

"Thirty-nine point five," Adrian corrected. "And drop that captain crap."

"Yeah, well, the thing of it is, the poor bastard caught his 39.5-pounder in June. The paper said he's all fucked up, waiting for the contest to end. He's sweating, hoping and praying someone doesn't bag a bigger one. Can't eat, can't sleep."

Jamey giggled. "Probably couldn't even get a decent chubby under that kind of pressure."

"Yeah," Terry answered. "Probably not good for shit, and I got a feeling we're going to ruin the poor bastard's life today."

"Let's just fish, Mr. Cairns," Adrian said. "If we catch your beast, it'll be by accident."

So we fished. Occasionally, Rorschach-like smudges showed up on Adrian's fish-finder, and he would call out a change of course. By 8:30, we'd been out for more than an hour. A couple of chinook salmon had hit our blue-and-silver Nasty Boy lures, but we'd caught nothing. The Cairns Bros. were getting impatient.

"Any fish left, Rhondo, or did you round 'em all up?" Terry said, reaching into his cooler for another Coors Light.

"Patience," Adrian counselled. "You always catch supper with me."

"Maybe we should change lures."

"Sure, Mr. Cairns. We can do that. We can do it your way, or we can catch fish."

At quarter to nine, Terry caught the first chinook salmon, a five-pounder. By half past, the Cairns Bros. bagged two more salmon and a rainbow trout, but nothing like the beast they were after. Then Jamey lost a poorly hooked fish. Just after 10, Terry stood up to a stagger. He wasn't hammered, but the beer wasn't helping his unsure sea legs. He took two steps forward before stumbling back. Adrian slid his sunglasses down his nose and winked up to me. That was his signal, his warning that someone was going to get sick.

The water was no longer still. We were drifting on a bit of a groundswell. The *Rip Tide*'s twin engines were almost idling while the 32-foot Trojan gently rolled and bounced, aggravating Terry's queasy innards. He fell to his knees, crawling to the stern to retch into the water. Jamey tried not to watch, but within a minute he was vomiting over the stern, too. I quietly snickered, seeing the brothers sprawled out on the deck, scratching at the boat's floor.

Jamey was the archetypal younger brother, softer than Terry, almost a sidekick. He only spoke after the big boy spoke, and, even then, his speech was an add-on to Terry's dialogue. So it seemed appropriate when he only started puking after seeing the belches shrieking out of his big brother's midsection. I wasn't sure whether it was beer or motion sickness. I looked down at the two men in their forties. They were a pathetic sight, hunched over, green like the smog over the SkyDome.

It was just as well that they were sick. It kept them occupied when we didn't get a hit for the next hour. The light wind and the strain on the taut fishing lines made this eerie sound, like whistles blaring in the distance, as waves slapped against the boat.

"Feeling better, Mr. and Mr. Cairns," Adrian said, interrupting their silence. "I hear it helps if you watch the horizon."

"Better," Terry said. "Good enough to start drinking again."

"Yeah, gonna get another Coors Beer," Jamey chimed in.

"You're not wanting to be doing that." Adrian smiled at Terry. "What about that new woman you told me about. Must be planning a fish-fry, or something, tonight. You'll want to keep yourself fresh."

"Nah, spent last night with Janet," Terry said with a boastful scratch.

"Again?" Jamey looked at his big brother. "You're seeing a lot of her. It's none of my business, but I just don't want to see you go through all that grief again."

"Nah, no paternity worries. Janet's like 51, and precisely 125 pounds. Good, firm ass. She doesn't want to knock herself up and bugger up her outfits. She just wants to go out. See, she married some rich wop. Dropped him out of sheer boredom."

"You're sure she's not after your money?"

"Jamey, Janet's just into having fun and going places. We're going to some artsy-fartsy musical in North York Friday, then to the Royal York."

"Just be careful, is all."

"Look, this chick goes Dutch on everything, and get this, her favorite song is 'My Way,' Sinatra's version. None of that Elvis shit. She's a woman after my own heart."

"I still prefer the interpretation of late Sid Vicious," I added.

The Cairns Bros. gave me this strange, contorted look, not so much at what I said, but because I actually spoke to them. I looked away to the stern where a rod was craning down toward the water.

"Hey… hey, we got… FISH ON… THREE O'CLOCK," I shouted.

The graphite trolling rod snapped back into the sun when the line slackened. Adrian ripped the rod from the holder, pulling up and rapidly reeling until the line stiffened. From the flying bridge, I watched a huge chinook salmon break the surface about a hundred feet out and pull down again, leaving *The Toronto Star* building in the background.

"Whoever's up, put on the fighting-belt," Adrian ordered.

Jolted from his post-beer breakfast throws, Jamey moved first, wrapping the adjustable plastic belt around his waist. Terry then steadied himself, grabbing Jamey's shoulder and ripping the belt from his brother's midsection.

"You got the last one," Jamey pouted.

"And you had the last hit, little brother," Terry said, fitting the belt to his own waist.

Adrian held the rod against his torso. "Put your sibling rivalry aside and settle this boys, or me and Jonzun will have this one for ourselves."

Terry stumbled forward to hold the rod's shaft. The reel wailed while the fish ran with the line, knifing a transparent streak into the lake. Terry Cairns frantically cranked the reel with his right hand, but the fish kept running, taking line the reel couldn't hold.

"He's losing too much string," Jamey said, "tighten the drag,"

"Do that and your brother will lose it." Adrian pointed at the water. "That fish has enough piss and vinegar to break our line. Jonzun, keep pulling this animal and tire him out."

With the shaft jutting out from the plastic belt, Terry sobered himself with thoughts of The Great Salmon Hunt. "What the hell do we have? Could this be our boy?"

"I won't say no, but land him before you put him on a scale," Adrian answered. "He's trying to make sure we get spooled right now."

"Already got your share spent on your uptown bitch, huh, brother?" Jamey sniffed.

"My share?" Terry scowled, reeling and pulling backwards. "If this is the freak I think it is, I'm afraid it's my fish and my cash, little guy."

"Oh, nice. I thought the plan was to split it no matter who pulled it in."

Terry grunted, pulling back more line and reeling more slack. "Sit down and shut up, little lady."

Jamey fell back into the starboard chair, crossing his arms, remaining dutifully silent like the bullied child he was.

"Mr. Cairns, keep the line tight… And Jonzun… Jonzun, bring us to a drift and then an easy tiptoe reverse." Adrian reeled in the last of the other five lines to avoid tangles. "Creep into the fish. Don't let him bugger around with the line. We don't need him taking any slack."

From the flying bridge, I could see we'd lost most of the line. There was maybe another 50 feet left. I brought the *Rip Tide* to a drift and slipped into reverse, crawling backwards.

Christ, even Adrian thinks these slobs might actually land the fish they're after, I thought.

I worked the boat as well as I could in reverse. Terry made up line quickly as we gained on his prize.

"Keep doing what you're doing, Jon," Adrian told me, "and a pinch starboard."

As ordered, I guided the boat slightly right. The fish was tiring, ailing from the wound to its mouth, the screaming expanding in its head from the terror of running from a pull it couldn't understand.

"Turn that crank nice and steady, Mr. Cairns," Adrian smiled. "Jonzun, our fish… He's going to get his second wind and run like a banshee when he sees our tub. Back off the reverse and drag him again before he sprints."

Terry stood reeling effortlessly until the fish came up again. It was more than three feet of glistening silver scales tiredly twisting and weaving. Just as Adrian said, the fish got its second wind, madly churning like a broken windmill from port to starboard and back again.

The fish was 20 feet from the boat when Adrian told Terry to step backwards. Dipping the net into the lake, he told Terry to reel steadily. The fish took a few more feet of line, but Terry kept hauling and pulling and reeling. The fish was too exhausted by then. There was a mad thrashing near the stern.

In an instant, Adrian's biceps tensed under his T-shirt. He lifted the netted animal out of the water and dropped it on the deck. Blood oozed from the wound the lure had carved, spearing through the top of its mouth. The fish opened and closed its mouth and huge gills, kicking out a sharp, clean sound by slapping its tail on the deck. But the beast's emotionless eyes refused to glaze over with pain as if its pride was at stake. It was the biggest, thickest salmon I'd ever seen.

"I'm not wanting you to get too excited," Adrian said. "But I think… Oh hell… This animal has to comfortably be 42 pounds."

"I told you this was our year," Terry cried. "Jamey, get the video going."

"No muscleman poses till I clobber it and kill it, Mr. Cairns."

Adrian slipped down below to retrieve his kill club, a wooden stick that was about a foot long, wrapped in steel at the end.

Terry spat. "I want footage of him alive. Go with the camera, little brother."

Jamey was out of his pout, gleefully running the camera while Terry reached into the net for his prize salmon. The barbed lure was still snarled in its jaws. Terry struggled with the salmon's gills while it bled on his sweats. He needed both hands to hold the fish out, raising it to the sky. The indignant salmon twisted in his grasp, madly flapping. I was climbing down from the flying bridge when I realized Terry had lost control.

"I told you to leave the fish alone," Adrian shouted from the hatch. "Put it on the deck and step on it till I get there. Where's my goddam kill club, Jonzun?"

In the next moments, the great fish curled slowly then rigidly straightened itself, slipping from Terry's grip. But it didn't hit the deck. Instead, the salmon's drop to the boat's hardwood floor stopped abruptly. The two open nasty boy barbs sank through Terry's No Fear T-shirt, ripping into his meaty stomach like the salmon had been mounted there. Terry's screaming filled the deck. His arms flailed and his legs danced a crude jig for the video. The salmon kept savagely whipping its head and tail.

"GET THIS FUCKER OFF ME," Terry screamed. His stuttered breaths blended with the sound of the wet fish ripping and bashing about on his chest. "PUT THE GODDAMN CAMERA DOWN, AND HELP ME, JAMEY."

The *Rip Tide*'s radio blurted out meaningless message just as Adrian emerged from the hatch and froze. Jamey and I were paralyzed, too. In the mad struggle, the weight and the hook and the fight continued ripping a gash deeper into Terry's stomach. Pieces of flesh peeked through his T-shirt.

Seemingly dancing four feet off the ground, the fish's mouth gasped open and shut, open and shut. It writhed through an angry air-swim in the midday sun. Terry grabbed at the fish as though it was a greased pig. He tried holding it by its slippery scales, and actually had his hands around the salmon's torso at one point. But the creature slipped away. In those last wild moments of resistance, the fish rolled, snapping open its mouth and exposing rows of tiny teeth. It bit down on the Nasty Boy lure, continuing to tear its mouth and Terry's chest, both of which were shredded.

It's trying to kill Terry Cairns, I thought.

Terry slapped at the salmon, sweeping it loose with his right hand.

We stood motionless as the fish fell from Terry's midsection, bleeding from its open mouth and twisting in the air. It fell onto the fading finish of the port rail with a dull thud, bouncing once off its top fin. Flipping onto its right side, the salmon's icy eyes never changed while it tumbled downward like a bent corkscrew. Its wide, silver tail swished upwards. The great salmon was falling back into the water. There was a splash. It was gone.

The only sound for the next several seconds was Terry's hoarse breathing. All four of us remained still, smelling the mix of fresh water, fuel, salmon, and Terry's blood. Interrupting his own tortured panting, Terry grabbed the net, stabbing it into the water. He was crying and stabbing. His screaming rants were littered with loud, angry grunts.

"He's gone, Mr. Cairns," Adrian said. "Sit down."

Terry Cairns hunkered back a step before letting his ass drop to the deck. Blood oozed through his white T-shirt and smeared his hands. The Nasty Boy lure was still stuck in his stomach, its barbs keeping a foothold in his flesh. A garbage bird swooped and squawked, grabbing a decaying piece of something from the lake's surface.

"Somebody pull this goddamn hook out of me," Terry seethed.

"I'll do no such thing, you're liable to spring a leak, sir," Adrian said, tossing a dusty first-aid box to Jamey. "Patch up your brother and leave that spike in him. They'll deal with it at the hospital."

Terry looked to the water with crinkled green eyes, bringing his cut forefinger to his mouth to taste his own blood. Over Terry's bitter murmurs, Adrian mumbled something about wanting these guys off the boat before one of them died. Terry's grumbling faded as I climbed to the flying bridge. My back ached when I sat down, easing the throttle forward.

I knew I had missed out on a pretty lavish tip, but I didn't care. I didn't want Terry to have that creature stuffed and painted and nailed to his wall. I didn't want him taunting the great salmon's corpse every morning over his greasy breakfast.

When I glanced over to *The Toronto Star* building, most of the smog had lifted, but there was still a faint green ring. I heard some snarling below and looked down to watch Terry pushing Jamey and string of gauze away with one hand while he held his bleeding stomach with the other. I thought about all the people I used to know, schlepping tables, working in offices, answering phones, typing for failing men like the Cairns Bros. I didn't know what I wanted to do. I wondered why everybody had to be something. I didn't know where I was going, and, for the first time, that seemed to be okay. Keep breathing, I told myself, keep sane, it's alright to stumble around and just get by for a while.

The summer was fading and Adrian would be laying me off in a few weeks. I didn't want to think about it. So I just let it go. Something will happen, I thought.

Maybe Mom was right. Maybe it was my rough patch. After all, I was poor. I didn't have any friends. And I was alone. But somehow, I was happy.

Alex Johnson walked to the beach bar carrying a sticky cinnamon roll on a saucer with one hand, making a peace sign with the other. *"Dos* expressos, *por favor."*

"Si." Vladimiro, the bartender, held up an index, nodding to Sondra Brooks as she sidled up next to Alex with a slim cigar in her mouth. *"Momento."* Vladimiro, producing a lighter, hit the butane, cupping his hands to light her Cohiba. "Same as smoked by *el presidente."* Stroking an imaginary beard, pointing at Sondra's stogy. "Only yours, lady size."

"Gracias," Sondra said. Watching Vlad pocket the lighter, go about the coffee drill, she waved at swirls of smoke as Alex picked up a pen from the bar, getting to work on a postcard. He hadn't but four or five words down when Sondra said, "What?"

Alex looked up, held a hand out, the pen. "What, what?"

"It's not 9:30. You, on a Caribbean beach with a lady 10 years junior, luckier than a Tomcat with two sacks of nuts, but already making the same face you did when that mystery meat—I said don't eat it—started repeating on you." Sondra dragged on her Cohiba. "I just want you to be happy, baby. It's our vacation."

Alex looked at her looking past him, watching the sun, blowing her cigar exhaust.

Ten years junior—ha. Sondra was a handsome lady, yeah, all that processed chestnut hair, almost natural except for the way the sun made it look over-sheened. And man was she wearing that swimsuit, a girl her age, toned. Same time, Alex was in better shape than anyone he knew, his age, gonna be 58. It'd be a pretty neat trick for her to do better, divorced more times than him. And what she trying to do back then? Start a new race? Yet there she was, classy lady like that, sucking on a stogie, making like he's damaged goods. Man, maybe this was too much too soon. Maybe they didn't know each other well enough to spend a week stranded on a Commie island with no shopping.

"Look," he said. "Bad enough I got Cecil chain smoking Exports, heavy, on the J-O-B, in the car. Now I got you." Waving a hand over the delicate floral print of her one-piece bathing suit. "Smoking a stogy same as Castro smokes."

Sondra bit gently, moving the cigar up and down in her mouth. "When in Santiago…"

But, as Alex pointed out, this wasn't even Santiago proper. Thirty clicks away, and Sondra didn't tell him about that. No, she just said she got a last-minute deal to go to Santiago—not the Mississauga of Santiago. Now here they were in the middle of Alex didn't know where. He had the heat rash, some kind of nasty business on the tops of his burnt feet, spent most of yesterday spraying the bowl until Sondra was able to score some black-market Imodium.

Again, Sondra said Alex shouldn't have ate that shit looked like Dr. Ballard's at the buffet. Yeah, she'd said so. Alex'd give her that. But now this was his first day of health proper, and he sees on CNN back in the room how they're having another revolution not a hundred miles away, Haiti. That was on top of the 600 Taleban 40-some miles away, Guantanamo, but then Sondra said the Taleban would be skinning white folks if they did get past the landmines. Fine, but she didn't tell Alex they'd be anywhere near the American base—landmines everywhere—that was his point. Besides, did she now mean to tell him she's a cigar smoker?

Sondra blew rings at him, said he didn't seem worried about any of that last night, at least not after the black-market Imodium kicked in and he took that shower that lasted two times.

Alex leaned away, seeing her on top of him. Yeah, she knew how to do it. Give her that, too. Plus, she'd brought those sexy safari outfits—cheetah, zebra—so he let the whole thing slide.

Took a bite out of his cinnamon bun, waving at the smoke as he consulted Sondra's pocket-sized English-to-Spanish phrase book, working on his postcard.

When the expressos arrived, both said *gracias*, Alex pushing two American singles at Vladimiro. Sondra, pointing down to the cinnamon bun, said, "What's that?"

Alex glanced at his plate. "Cinnamon sprinkle."

"No." More specific with her index this time, that speck right there. "I mean, what is that?"

"Another cinnamon sprinkle."

"Then why's it moving, baby?"

Rather than risk closer inspection, Alex pushed the plate to Vladimiro's side of the bar, telling Vlad to clean his shit up, standards. That he, Alex, ought to ask for his two Americano dollars back, every one of them trying to give him dengue fever. Vladimiro said *si*, but Alex wasn't supposed to bring outside food to the bar. Alex said there wasn't a goddamn shop for a half-hour, that he got the bun from the buffet at breakfast, that this was all part of the same hotel. Vlad said *si*, but Alex still wasn't supposed to bring in any outside food.

Alex let it slide, again, sipping his expresso while he looked over the postcard, adding points of punctuation here and there, addressing it.

"That guy." Sondra chin-pointed at a man with a tiny metallic RCA camcorder a few tables over. "German over there."

Alex looked. "Mr. Norbert?"

"Think Norbert's his given name."

"Whatever." Alex talked as he edited. "Man from East Berlin, the one you're talking. Met him right about here night before last. Says he's been coming here ever since before the wall came down on account of this was the only hot-spot allowed to Commies going way back—Mr. Norbert."

"Right, you see what he's doing?"

Alex lowered his head, looking over his sunglasses at his Mr. Norbert, then down to the beach, a few topless French and German ladies scattered amongst some Canadians. "Just a dirty old man. Lonesome. Maybe a pecker puller, is what he is, maybe."

"You think we should say anything?"

"Uh-uh, no." Alex pushed his glasses back up his nose. "Cause an international incident."

"But you're a cop, Fraud. You can't just look the other way."

"That's right." Alex extended a thumb. "Only that's back in Toronto." Adding an index. "This being a police state of its own— twitchy Hispanic boys with bad skin at both ends of the complex toting little Russian handguns from the '60s—I'm a wee bit, hmm, out of my jurisdiction."

"Jurisdiction, give me a break."

Alex, adding another finger, said, "Also, Mr. Norbert isn't committing no fraud, so far as I can see, and Fraud doesn't do pervs. Like I say, just a dirty old East German man taking video of half-naked ladies gonna splice 'em together, wank to it when he gets home, memories of the island. Aside of which, like you said, I am on vacation."

Sondra, motioning an open hand down to the beach. "All those ladies—they don't know."

"I'm telling you, let it slide." Alex took another sip, looking at the bottom of his cup, coagulated sugar. "Little cup of coffee like this, you'd think they'd at least fill it to the rim."

"It's café de Cuba," Sondra said, saying it like the locals— *Cooba*. "You, expecting a double-double, here."

"*Cooba*," Alex said, mimicking her. "Goddamn *Coobans* got but one kind of coffee, extra strong, one size. You saw how Vladimiro looked at me on day one when I asked could he please make me a latte, like he never heard of such a delicacy." Holding up Sondra's phrase book. "Spanish don't even seem to have a word for it, latte."

Squinting, Sondra cast her gaze to this Norbert with the camcorder again. "You really don't think we should say anything? You know that shit he's recording going end up on the same website as that guy got caught taking movies of ladies going pee at the Eaton Centre."

"Don't you show 'em your ta-tas—like, what, you gonna get 'em tanned?—don't you worry." Alex shook his head. "And not a word, vacation. Last thing I want is confrontation, everyone so touchy these days, especially the French on account of they're so worried everyone's trying to dilute their culture. Just put it in your back pocket in case we need it later. Let it slide."

"Put it in my pocket? So we pretend we just don't see what he's doing?"

"Like you said." Alex stroked an imaginary beard, copying Vladimiro. "When in Santiago… Just let it play out on its own. I mean, these people been looking the other way ever since the missile crisis, so let's us let it slide, too. This is not our country."

Leaning over, he signed the postcard, re-reading it.

"Who you writing to, consulting my phrase book like a diplomat."

"Cecil."

"Cecil? Your partner? Thought this was your vacation from him. Thought you hate him, that he hate you."

"Don't hate Cecil—I never said that—just feel better when I'm here and he's there on account of Chief Inspector Almano can't finally blame me next time Cecil takes a cellphone upside a tourist in a case of mistaken identity."

"So why you writing him?"

"Rattle his cage on account of he told me not to send him anything from Cuba. Said he gets mail from here, he probably ends up on some kind of cross-reference Commie-CIA-CSIS list, fuck up his career later on."

Sondra said, "Sounds like he's doing a job of that himself." She smiled at Alex, his closely-cropped white walls—his body lean from paying two alimonies, walking wherever he could to save on the rising cost of gas. "Let me see what you're writing him."

"Nothing about you."

Sondra pursed, waving at herself. "Just let me see."

Alex licked his lips, handed the postcard over. She took it, looking at the black-and-white photo, circa 1961, a young Fidel Castro with a rifle slung over his shoulder, leading fellow revolutionaries through a path in the mountains somewhere near here. Flipping it over, seeing Alex had addressed it to the poor white boy care of headquarters, 40 College Street, she read the inscription.

Dear Companero *Cecil Bolan,*

As you can see, we are closing in on the American sektor. el Presidente *is wielding his rifle like* el nino, *leading by example & giving new life to the* Revolución. *Nights have been cool, days hot & long. Fortunately* cerveza *ain't but a buck, plentiful & strong.* De tadaos modos, *as we move on to nearby Guantanamo to finally evict the Imperialist* Yanquis *(their lease done expired in 2002), I thank you for your regular* inteligente. *With comrades like you throughout the so-called free world,* Viktory *will soon be ours.*

In solidarity, Che Guevara Jr. III

Sondra looked up. "Is there even a Che III?"

Alex said there must be, that Che had a bunch of kids he didn't feel sorry about leaving poor when he resigned from Castro's cabinet and went off to stir up his Marxist shit elsewhere, the Congo, then Bolivia where the army got him, did biblical shit. Took his pipe, tied him up, posed him for pictures, the mocking, then shot up his arms and legs, waited for him to bleed out, die. How the fuck did Alex know that? On account of he read about it. Oh yeah, Sondra wanted to know, where did he read that Che didn't feel bad for leaving his kids poor? Alex pointed over his shoulder, the lobby. The lobby? That's right, same place where he bought the postcard, they were selling copies of Che's resignation letter, two

American dollars. Alex was reading it, in Che's hand, and right there Che said he didn't feel bad about leaving his kids nothing on account of he knew the state would provide for them. Aside from that, Cecil wouldn't know whether there was a Che III, that Cecil was young, white, and dumb. Main thing was Cecil was getting a Commie postcard at work implying he was a Commie, and that Alex would be back to see the look on his face by the time it got cleared by Havana and sent to Cecil at headquarters in Toronto.

"Why do you play with him so, get him riled?"

Hmm, Alex thought it over a few seconds, said, "On account of I'm in the autumn of my career and I have to work with a boy-man needs so much seasoning." Rising from the bar, pulling an aqua towel—had to leave a $20 deposit on that thing—off the stool behind him, over his shoulder, he led Sondra downstairs to the beach, setting up under a bamboo umbrella. Sondra said it was called a *palapa*.

Despite a day out of the sun on account of the mystery meat, Alex was still a little crispy. He was worried that maybe he had some kind of nasty fungal thing festering on the tops of his elevens, having avoided Sondra's warning of the ozone on day one, so he wore socks under his sandals, a red pair of light weight cotton karate pants and a long-sleeved T-shirt that said MEDIC on the front, red cross with a stick man in the middle.

Leaning back in his lounge, the headrest fell back a couple notches—klunk, klunk—Alex thinking goddamn Soviet workmanship as he watched white caps crashing against the reef horse-shoeing the beach.

It was getting hotter, little crabs digging themselves out from the under the sand, looking at Alex with their antenna eyes, rushing out to sea for the day. Fascinated, he watched their exodus, asking Sondra what did she think of the place, the food?

She said the hotel was basic, pretty alright, the food plain, mostly, hearty, truck-driver breakfasts. But in addition to that aforementioned shit looked like Dr. Ballard's, what were they thinking with the calamari? Yeah, uh-huh, Alex knew what she was talking about, squid in brown gravy—yuck. Damn Cubans still hadn't figured out how to cook seafood on account of too much Russian influence—shoddy Soviet workmanship again. And what the fuck was it with these chaise lounges? As soon as you rest your head, it went klunk, klunk down a down a couple notches. What good was that?

As for the complex itself, Sondra said it was a jewel in the jungle. They were in the middle of nowhere, sure, but it was a national park, and could Alex believe those screech owls the first night?

Yeah, he admitted, it was kind of a kick seeing mom and dad teaching junior to fly, junior crash landing in the palms. And look at that, he said, turning around, some poor Hispanic goat on the edge of the cliff, yelling at them—bah, bah. But what was with the vampires? Just garden-variety vegetarian bats living inside the cliffs, Sondra said, pointing at the overhangs 200 feet above, the holes.

Also, did Alex hear what the guy said at breakfast, that it was Club Bucanero's 16th anniversary? That's why they were having a regatta. But, watching buff Cuban boys swim supplies out to a rustic vessel, Alex said there was only one boat and he was pretty sure it was confiscated during the Bay of Pigs. He watched a woman's sandy-blonde head emerge from under the water, revealing a bikini that was too tight on her substantial lower half.

"Nice dainties on that Conçois," Sondra said.

Alex said, "You know why she do that, right?"

"What? Wears them panties too tight?"

"Yeah. Like, she think, if she wears tight bottoms no one will notice how generous, but solid, her hindparts are."

"Got a butt on her, no hiding that."

On the edge of the surf, Conçois tried to remove her sea socks, necessary equipment as the surf here was more rocky than sandy. But a nice wave knocked her down, Conçois scrambling on all fours until she found her footing. Grabbing at her sea socks again, flinging them one by one on the sand, she reached behind her back for her bikini string, pulling it.

Still a little unaccustomed to this sort of emancipation, Alex looked away as soon as he saw those nip-ons, first to Sondra staring at the same thing, then the woman's husband. He shot Alex a dirty look, sour. Alex smirked, thinking fuck it, looking back at Conçois, speaking to Sondra.

"Goddamn, now Beaumont's eyeballing me."

"The husband?" Sondra looked sideways at Beaumont, turning to Alex, then Conçois. "He is." Back to Alex. "Tell him to tell her put a top on, he doesn't want anyone to see."

"I know it," Alex said. "But it's going to be an international incident. I just know that, too. Asides, you were saying something different about Mr. Norbert, the German, just a few minutes gone by ago."

Sondra looked up at the beach bar, said, "Only Norbert's taping the French lady's got no top and a big butt. You, you're just looking, and I can't hardly look away myself, them too-small panties on her large hips like one of those underground cartoons by the guy did that Keep on Truckin' decal. How do you say, 'My eyes, my eyes,' *español*?"

Alex said he didn't know, for Sondra to check her phrase book.

Conçois was shaking the water out of her hair when Beaumont, in his little cabana trunks, dull green and blue stripes, appeared in front of Alex. "If you don't mind, my wife is, how you say *timide*—self-conscious."

"*Timide*?" Alex looked sideways at Sondra covering her mouth, back to Beaumont, then leaned right so that he could see Conçois, now smoothing her hair back, perky little breasts pointing into the sun. "You sure you have the right word? Looks pretty self-assured to me. How do you mean, self-conscious?"

Beaumont shifted bare feet in the hot white sand, said, "What you are doing is *impoli*."

Impoli? With Sondra mum, letting it slide, Alex tried to think of what to say next, something about how blocking his view was *impoli*. Like, this was a public beach, at least for folks from out of town, made it okay to look on account of Conçois shaking her ta-tas right in front of him. What? Should he, Alex, tuck a fin into her too-small panties? Was that what Beaumont wanted, a tip?

But before Alex worked up the courage to say any of that, Sondra was speaking up on his behalf. Saying, "Listen, Beaumont, I can't avoid looking at your lady, and I am a slave to the joystick, thanks. Besides, what would you do if I told you some dirty old East German is videotaping your wife right now?"

"East German?" Beaumont looked around. "I'd, how you say *agrafe*? Oh yes, I would staple his eyes shut. Where is this man, this East German taping my wife?"

Beaumont followed Sondra's index up to the shirtless bald guy, Norbert focusing 20 or 30 feet in front of them, Conçois' torso beading water.

And with that, Beaumont was off, yelling shit *le merde*, something about *scheisse* films, while Alex watched Conçois tying her hair behind her head, taking her time, seemingly oblivious to everything around her, except, of course, the Cuban sun.

"Look at Beaumont now." Sondra said. "Got Norbert against the railing, taking his recorder away. Look at him."

"Told you you'd cause an international incident." Alex lowered his head, peered over his glasses, then pushed them back up his nose, his eyes following Conçois back to her lounge, leaning back when her head fell down a couple notches—klunk, klunk—shoddy Soviet workmanship again.

"I said look at Beaumont." Sondra couldn't believe it. "Not his wife."

Alex smiled slightly, followed Sondra's gaze upstairs, Beaumont holding Norbert with one hand, looking into the camera with the other, trying to see what Norbert had been recording. Back to Beaumont's half-naked wife, Alex said, "Good thing I made sure you didn't say anything when we first noticed, like I said. Held onto it until we could use it."

"We." Sondra looked up to the bar, Vladimiro interceding between the German and the Parisian now, trying to keep the peace, then back to Alex watching Conçois, again. "Looks like everywhere, somebody's getting away with something, huh?"

Alex smiled, said, "Looks like it."

Sondra sat up, eyeballing Alex, the way he was taking in the sight of Conçois oiling up, and said, "Hey bitch, want a job?"

Victor Elias breaks an egg-shaped pill in half, more or less, with his thumbnail, then returns the slightly larger portion to its amber bottle. Washing the smaller half down with a couple gulps of lukewarm tap water, he rinses the measuring cup too quickly to really clean it, placing it upside down on the dish rack. Ritual complete, he sits on a chipped maple chair someone next door mistook for trash, cradling his head in his hands, waiting for his medicine to do its thing.

Near his feet, a longhaired salt-and-pepper cat named Saul Goldberg licks himself at speeds exceeding 1,800 licks an hour. Victor knows this because he has clocked Saul at more than 30 licks over a one-minute period. Just to be sure, Victor does the math again on the back on his phone bill. Struggling with the zeros before locating a solar-powered calculator in his desk's third drawer, punching the appropriate digits.

"Thirty times 60," he whispers, barely moving his lips, hitting the equal sign. "Eighteen-hundred."

Satisfied he has roughly re-confirmed Saul's speed, Victor finds himself counting things he loves in his sparse bachelor. A pine bookcase that's been in the family for years is lined with binders containing unused samples, mostly pristine, of every stamp produced by Canada Post since 1973—save for the bowhead whale, circa 1979, endangered species series. More than 600 CDs are scattered in stacks of various heights on milk crates and lamp tables. Five paintings depicting various outdoor scenes by local artists of little renown dot four sandstone walls.

As for the furniture, Victor is not the first owner of a single stick, not even the blue wine-bottle lamp that's simply in bad taste. The kitschy Ricky Ricardo bed that folds out of his wall—

called a Murphy bed—came with the place. Victor had to pay a deposit on that thing, which seems odd now that he thinks of it. What, are they afraid he's going to dismantle it, steal it? How would he even get that contraption out of here?

Lately, Victor's been getting the shakes if he doesn't have a half egg-shaped pill every three or four days. His is not yet a nasty habit, but indeed, he has been taking the half-pills more often. Making a mental note of it, he is nonetheless pleased by the onset of a blissfully predictable brain rub he likes to call mental floss.

He picks himself up, takes three steps to a door inconveniently located off the kitchen, stooping to look into a framed mirror and blinking playfully at his heavy lids. He runs a hand through the simulated part down the middle of his hair as a matter of routine, training a new haircut, reaching for the brown lambskin car coat dangling alone on a rack made of game-used Maple Leafs sticks— Kaberle, Tucker, Belak, and Corson.

Dad thought the hockey-stick coat rack was kind of neat, that it'd be valuable one day. Poor dad didn't understand that once you altered a collectible, you destroyed its value. Still kind of neat, Victor tells himself.

Throwing on his lambskin coat, opening the door, he lets himself into the hall and locks three deadbolts, one of which came with the place. Heads to the elevator from there, pressing the down arrow with one of his keys, wiping it on his blue corduroys, germs, before his ride arrives.

Inside, the Muzak version of "Noël" is piped through invisible overhead speakers as Victor presses L with the end of the same key, wiping it on his pants again. Cursing like the original Popeye, filthy, when the box heads up one floor to 11, knowing enough to smile politely as the doors open.

"Was feeling kind of down until right now," some old guy in a grey bubble coat says. Stepping inside, standing too close, he does the zipper up to his ears. "But that smile of yours, that's just the pick-me-up I needed. Beautiful as a morning glory in late August, maybe even more beautiful."

Aware he should've had had braces, in his youth, Victor knows old guy is lying. "Thanks," he says anyway, awkwardly covering the slight gap between his front teeth with his left hand. "Thank you."

"Hammond." Old guy paws at his curly hair roughly matching the color of his coat, bringing his right hand down, extending it, forcing it into Victor's. "Ray Hammond, 1138."

"Victor," Victor says, dropping his left to expose those teeth. "Nice to meet you."

Holding the grip too long, Ray says, "You new here?"

"No." Victor, noticing the elevator doors still open, withdraws his right with a twitch, pressing L for lobby, sending the elevator into descent. "There." Looking at his sensible work boots with the green patch, he diverts his eyes, noting that this Ray is wearing white Rockports, out of season. Nice pants, too—black velour drawstrings—and he's talking again.

"How long is it you say you've lived here?"

"Three years," says Victor. Still looking down, studying the tiles, pointing. "Hey, that isn't terracotta. It's only supposed to look like terracotta."

"Three years?"

"Yes." Victor takes a deep breath and looks at old guy for a sign. "Three years now."

"Well, I've been here five." Ray holds out an open palm. "And I would have noticed you. What unit are you in?"

Victor doesn't really want to answer but finds himself saying 1027 anyway. He doesn't want to answer any of the other questions, either. But, as they leave the elevator for the lobby, then the building, it appears Ray is also heading west on Carlton. "So what do you do?" he says.

"Landscaper," Victor replies. "Plant trees, level lawns, throw white or red stones where people are tired of cutting their lawns.

Landscaper."

"For whom?"

"It's the off-season. Too early to say."

"Oh, I'm sure things will turn right around for you, with a smile like that, money."

"Again." Victor scratches the hairline scar running through his left brow. "It's the off-season."

Against the sedative effect, Ray talks at Victor. And he does it too fast, creating a hyper-blue blur that Victor can't keep up with as his mental floss takes full effect. He's simply trying to put one foot in front of the other—looking out for patches of black ice camouflaged by the fresh flurries—as Ray turns right with him through an alley. Then west again through a parking lot near Maple Leaf Gardens.

By now, Ray knows that Victor was born in Welland, that he has family there. Albeit vague, it still seems like too much information, so Victor tries to change pace as they cross Church Street.

"You don't ever hear me making noise up there, do you?" he says abruptly.

"No." Ray smiles, finally getting somewhere. "Why? What are you doing down there?"

Disliking the new direction as much as the last, Victor backpedals. "Sometimes I have a few drinks, play the music too loud. I like Louis Prima. And the music, it carries into the court-yard, you know?"

"So you like to 'Enjoy Yourself'?" Ray says, eyes wide, hanging on. "You like to party?"

"Not really," Victor says. "Just a couple of beers a couple times a month. Sometimes I play the Louis Prima too loud. That's all."

"You like beer?"

"I go out drinking about once a month." Victor catches himself doing that thing he does when he lies, bringing his thumb to the corner of his mouth, wiping at nothing. "That's about all I can afford during the off-season."

"Well, if you want beer," Ray says, "I've got a case and a half of Old Vienna upstairs."

"Thanks, I'm good."

"It's okay." Ray shakes his head, moving sideways behind the arena. "Tell me when you're coming up and I'll have it ready for you."

"Let's meet down the road on this one," Victor says.

"Look." Ray is walking backwards now, facing Victor. "It's okay. Just let me just tell you the reason why I'm doing this. I had bought the beer for a friend who was coming in from out of town. From Montreal. I had a visitor. I was going to have a visitor coming in from Montreal and then he couldn't make it. Just so you know the reason why I'm doing this."

"Thanks." Victor waves him off. "Some other time."

"It's just because of your situation—that's the reason why I'm doing this. Come by anytime. I'm not going to drink it."

Victor says nothing, biting down.

"What?" Ray's mouth hangs open, eyes filled with concern like that picture in the paper of Winona Ryder being sentenced to three-years probation. "Guy can't buy another guy a beer? Something wrong with that, Victor?"

"No, I just—"

"You just what? Why is it weird I want to buy you a beer? What does it say to you?"

Victor pulls his chin to his collarbone, pointing a tan leather work glove. "It wouldn't be weird if you wanted to buy me a beer." Side-stepping Ray, taking a few backward steps north. "But you want to buy me 36 beers. Who buys someone 36 beers? That means something, so what does it mean? Is it like having a yellow hankie in your back pocket? Code for you like getting pissed on? Something like that?"

***

Tuesday morning, laundry day during the off-season, Victor sorts whites and colors. Eventually, he decides to just do colors because he doesn't want to lug the bleach downstairs. Doesn't want to spill it on the colors again.

As he unlocks the three deadbolts, a wintergreen envelope falls to his feet from between the cracks. The name Vince is scrawled in black ink across the front. Opening it anyway, Victor feels moist glue, meaning it hasn't been there long, spitty. An overstated steeple sits in the background, captured among dozens of pine trees. Pieces of green glitter stick to Victor's fingers as he opens the card. Smells like aftershave, or something, musk. Inside the name Vince is scribbled in again, prefacing a printed greeting.

To wish you the blessing of peace and happiness at Christmas time and always.

Beneath, written in ink:

Remember you are welcome any time you get the urge for that beer at my place.

Your neighbor, Ray, Suite 1138

"Thirty-six beers," Victor mumbles. "Thirty-six beers."

***

Two days before Christmas, Victor holds a black duffel bag with gold piping, waiting for the elevator while 1021 shares his theory on global warming. He speaks slowly so Victor can understand, explaining how this, too, is connected to the Taleban when the doors open to "O Little Town of Bethlehem."

Walking into a plume of musk, both men recoil slightly at Ray Hammond. Thinking Old Spice, Victor drops his bag. He can see that Ray's been too much in the tanning bed. He's red like an onion and his teeth are too white—bleaching—and he has Victor pushed up against the buttons. "You get my Christmas card?" Smells like he's been drinking, too. Gin.

"Yes." Victor smiles nice, tasting something he's only supposed to smell. "It's lovely, especially the sparkles. Thanks. Thank you. Merry Christmas."

"Did I get your name right? Vince?"

Victor is tempted to lie, say yes, keep it simple. Worried, however, that 1021 might have better information, he politely makes the correction. "No, it's Victor. Easy mistake."

Ray extends his hand. "Let's try again."

Victor obliges and Ray holds him, bringing his left mitt to rest on top of Victor's right forearm, noticing his duffel bag on the elevator floor. "Going to see your family?"

"Yes, family."

"And they are where again?"

Victor sighs, removing his hand from Ray's grip, crossing his arms to create space, bumping an elbow into Ray's chest. "Welland."

"Welland?" Ray holds his ground, maintaining eye contact. "How long?"

"Just a couple days. Two and a half."

"Oh." Ray drops his face when the doors open out to the lobby. "Just a couple days in Welland? Two and a half? That's all?"

"Yes." Victor grabs his bag, turns sideways, working his way around Ray and out of the box. "That's all."

Following, Ray says, "Something happen at home?"

Victor waves over his shoulder. "Merry Christmas."

"Any time you want that beer. I've still got that case and a half of OV sitting up there. And did I tell you the reason why I'm doing this?"

"Merry Christmas," Victor says again, breaking for the door in long, important strides.

"It's just because of your situation. That's the reason, the reason why I'm doing this."

***

First thing December 26th, Victor climbs onto a Greyhound back to Toronto. Wears sunglasses even though it's overcast, hoping for sleep. Eight or nine rows behind the driver, he fidgets his right index into the fifth pocket of his jeans, hooking a half-pill with his nail, pulling it into his palm.

Victor eyes the driver in the rearview and fakes a yawn, depositing the half-pill in his mouth. When the driver looks away, Victor unscrews the top of his water bottle and gulps down what he believes to be half a cup, taking his mental floss as prescribed.

Sitting back, he removes a sealed case containing the 35-cent bowhead whale stamp from his shirt pocket, grading its condition in his head. Figures it's excellent, excellent plus. That it would've been near mint if it wasn't for the ding in the upper right corner. Then he wonders what Robert Bateman was thinking with the not-quite-full-on angle. If Bateman was a credible naturalist, Victor figures he would've painted the bowhead in such a way as to put the beast on display. That's what he should have done—profiled the fish. Yeah, since most people had never seen a bowhead in the real, Victor included, Victor thinks Bateman should've painted the whole damn whale instead of obsessing over domain. Deciding dad must've paid about 20 bucks, at least 10 too much, Victor slides the case back into his shirt pocket, wondering how many bowheads are left.

He is serene by the time the bus climbs the Skyway over Hamilton, almost aroused. For the first time, he finds beauty in the stacks of industry, disappointment when the view is gone. After that, it's a maze of highways and cars and trucks and speaking billboards and concrete and brown patches of dead grass all the way to the downtown Toronto terminal on Bay.

A \$7.75 cab ride later—oh hell, Victor's telling the driver to keep both fives, Happy Holidays—he's in his building and in the elevator, relieved to be alone, listening to Muzak's "Frosty the Snowman" until the doors open at his floor.

Down the hall, he unlocks the three deadbolts and lets himself into his kitchen. Drops the black duffel bag on the floor, allows his car coat to slide off his body and over the duffel bag.

Shuffling a few steps to the fridge, almost outside himself, he grabs an Old Vienna, twists off the cap, takes a swallow. Wiping his mouth on his sleeve of his cable turtleneck when he notices that paintings of five local artists of little renown are not dotting his sandstone walls. Binders protecting his stamps no longer line the pine bookcase, which is also gone. As are the 600 some CDs that were stacked in piles of various heights. The campy foldout bed, the Murphy, has been stripped from the wall. Saul Goldberg is not at his feet licking at a rate of 1,800 licks an hour. The hockey stick coat rack that wasn't going to be worth anything—Victor guessed it, also taken. And there isn't anything to sit on, either.

Save for the wine-bottle lamp and a few dozen paperbacks scattered on his desk, the place is empty.

Looking back in his refrigerator, trying to remember where he got the money to buy all this OV when it's not even his brand, Victor sees six neat rows of brown bottles. Counting six in each row, save for the row he took one from, which now has five, he goes for the third drawer in his desk. Finding the calculator missing, he allows himself to trust his times-tables.

"Thirty-six beers," he whispers. Lowering himself onto the floor, sitting in a position resembling the lotus, cradling his head. Wondering why, trying to remember exactly what that Ray told him, whether Ray had actually said the reason why he was doing this. "Thirty-six beers."

Natalia Cauzillo wasn't running late this morning. Not at first, not until she spotted a burnt roach. It was sitting on the edge of a rusted storage crate, the one that passes for her coffee table.

Even after she lit up and salvaged a hit, sucking the smoke out like sweet poison, she still could have made it in by nine. But with a tattoo of drums needling the buzzing bass on her stereo, minutes checked themselves off, bringing on nagging thoughts and questions and images.

With each note, she silently begged for an end to her routine, or at least a desert sanctuary renting out escape by the hour. She felt like she was doing something wrong. Figured she had to be, because every minute of her own seemed to be wasting into nothingness.

Half-heartedly wondering what organs to sign over for the day they became priceless, she licked her rosary, hitting pause and hearing an electronic click freeze insistent rhythms. In the next instant, she was pushing more buttons, seven more to be precise. On the other end, another phone started ringing. Damien answered halfway through the second jingle.

"Systems," he mumbled, substituting the department for a hello.

She tried to sound frazzled when she needn't. "Hi Damien. It's Natalia and I... I—"

"Hi Nat," he said, interrupting her, his voice smiling.

She hesitated, said, "Yeah, hi. Look, Damien, my morning, it's off. It's... The fire alarms went haywire in the night."

"So you're just phoning in late before you are? Good plan."

"Yeah, tell Gina, but only if you need to."

"Not to worry," he assured her. "This'll keep her at bay for...

Should by you an hour."

She breathed sharply. "K. See you in a bit. Thanks, Damien."

"Nat?"

She gritted her teeth, closing her eyes tightly, pressing the phone against her head until it hurt. She hated it when they called her Nat, and Damien had done it twice now. "Yeah?"

"Try sponge stoppers for your ears next time." It sounded like he was standing, wanting so damn badly to be helpful. "Next time that happens with the fire alarms, try sponge stoppers."

"K, thanks Damien," she said, the dismissal presenting itself in her voice. "See you."

"K, bye."

Cute little alpha geek, she thought, hanging up and swooping down on the pause button. In a millisecond, the stereo erupted from where it left off, sending out something even Damien's stoppers couldn't have stopped.

Natalia sat on the couch, adjusting her blood-red smoking jacket, a second-hand gem doubling as her robe. Carefully rolling, she wetted the cigarette papers down with dabs of saliva, twisting the skinny end. Satisfied, she placed the fresh joint on the floor heater to flash-dry.

A stride away, she was dancing to the cassette on her stereo. She bought the tape from a kid busking up at the corner last Saturday. He said it wasn't like the acoustic stuff he was playing that day. Natalia nodded while he went on about his band. She hadn't asked. Didn't care. Didn't even bother sliding the tape into her deck until this morning. More than anything, she just liked the idea of some strange kid making music in his basement with obsolete machines.

There was no agenda, just an experiment of influences on a morning when she needed something of her own. More discord than harmony, it was music without a message, music without words, music that related to the concept of nothingness. Driving and calming at once, it pillaged from surf-au-go-go, jazz, techno, industrial, disco, and a bit of funk. She didn't know what to call it. She just played it, played it loud, and kept playing it when it was time to stop dancing, time to light her homemade cigarette, then time to dance some more.

Four or five pulls in, her warm face pulsed in red throbs, the bass pounding her insides faster than her heart. Natalia liked the feeling of her smoking jacket coming undone. She was high on real and imaginary crystalline threads as much as she was simply high. Soft light seemed to glow in the mirror while she whipped her matted morning hair around in time to the very imperfect blend of retro and contemporary.

Running a hand down the length of her right leg, those next steps were the beginnings of a selfish sidewalk dance designed to entrap only her. She was spinning—muscles flexing—and taking campy Polaroids with the camera in her head. The smoking jacket was somewhere on the floor, and she was licking her rosary again, slowing down, drifting.

"Anywhere," she said, looking into the mirror and taking herself in her arms.

***

It's 10:45 now. The paper says salt relieves fatigue, but Natalia Cauzillo doesn't believe it. She's at her desk, and nobody's acting out of sorts, probably because she called in late before she was. Being late, that's not her pattern, not yet.

She didn't get paranoid until she took the elevator a few minutes ago. She started hearing something she wasn't really hearing. Even then she knew she wasn't really hearing it, because it was music—real music.

Natalia Cauzillo is stoned now. But it's too early to be stoned, so they probably think she's bagged, that she couldn't sleep after the bells went off last night. Could be they think she's just hungover, which is still better than being stoned, for some reason. Or maybe they know they're killing her softly and quietly admiring her rate of decay.

Sunday afternoon, she was the one to get the call, so she worked a few more of her own private hours, straightening out the mess some well-meaning cyberpunk made on the website. Then it was 17 straight on Monday, keeping an aging system up and running, four or five hours sleep by the time she came down, then back in at 8:30 Tuesday morning. Last night, she crashed somewhere around seven, sleeping until somewhere around seven this morning, and she's still tired.

They've told her how to dress, how to act, that there's seldom enough time for lunch. They've suggested that she smile broader and wider. As for the hours, she knew there'd be too many. They had been clear about that during the interview process.

Sometimes, like today, she's getting some of the time back, some of the time that belonged to her in the first place—time to think, time to get off, and time to dance to a hazy, narcotic cop-out. But there's never enough space to go over it, never enough to feel much of anything. Just a taste, that's all she ever gets—a taste.

By now, her unnatural smile has been exchanged with Damien, Gina, and Romy. It's quiet, too quiet, so quiet that it's uncomfortable. There's no banter among these virtual people, nothing to laugh at, either. Natalia's pretty sure it's against one of the new policies mounted and framed on the walls in Helvetica.

In the white noise of office silence, she can barely hear hail clicking a nearby window like tangerine fingernails, which is probably just as well. She'll be back soon enough, sitting in a fake room walled off from everything and everyone. The blue-green hue on the mainframe in front of her will be filled with a mirage of letters and codes and key words and back slashes. Although moments in time will be missing, an updated 1950s-style pinup calendar will mark the space as hers.

The important thing is that she's not here right now, not really, not at all. The pains shooting through her wrists are gone. Her throat doesn't feel so gritty, and her eyes have stopped throbbing, too.

Natalia Cauzillo is dancing. Somewhere in her head she's still in her living room, stepping on her blood red smoking jacket. Soft on her feet, she's doing that lewd sidewalk dance, wishing she was driving too fast into a yellow-and-paisley-blue sun on her last ride out.

The busker who made the sounds, he's with her; their bodies an animated sculpture blending music and ideas with human petrol. They dance on the agitated dance floor. Craning their necks, twirling like skaters, creating a blur of circles, and dreaming and dreaming and dreaming, even if it doesn't mean anything at all. Neither wonders about the plainclothed prowling the edges of their circle. They are part of the same production, just like every-one else, hiding and balancing and taking themselves in their very own arms when they'd rather not be so alone.

About the Author

Vern Smith is the author of *The Green Ghetto* (Run Amok Books), a novel set on Detroit's dysfunctional prairie. *Broken Pencil* calls it "a model for modern westerns." His fiction has appeared in several anthologies and magazines, most recently *Corporate Catharsis* (Paper Angel Press) and *BULL*. His novelette, *The Gimmick*, was a finalist for Canada's highest crime-writing honor, the Arthur Ellis Award. A veteran of four daily newspapers, three magazines, two radio stations, and one government caucus, he is a native of Windsor, Ontario and a longtime resident of Toronto. Since immigrating to the U.S., he has lived on the edge of Chicago in quasi-rural Illinois where the streets are named after dead golfers. Coincidentally, he has just wrapped a novel about a caddy pulling a payroll heist. It is called *Under the Table* and will be published by Run Amok Books.